Also by Robert B. Gillespie

The Last of the Honeywells
Empress of Coney Island
The Hell's Kitchen Connection
Heads You Lose
Print-Out

DEATH-STORM

ROBERT B. GILLESPIE

Carroll & Graf Publishers, Inc.
New York

Copyright © 1990 by Robert B. Gillespie
All rights reserved

First Carroll & Graf edition 1990

Carroll & Graf Publishers, Inc
260 Fifth Avenue
New York, NY 10001

Library of Congress Cataloging-in-Publication Data

Gillespie, Robert B.
    Deathstorm / Robert B. Gillespie. — 1st ed.
      p.   cm.
    ISBN: 0-88184-582-5 : $15.95
    I. Title.
  PS3557.I3795D4   1990
813'.54—dc20   90-1677
                                                                                        CIP

Manufactured in the United States of America

I. Firestorm

1.

Late afternoon, late August, Fred Engelhart stepped out on the cantilevered deck of his shoreline house. Clad only in white canvas shorts, he shielded his eyes from the wind and sun like a little boy saluting, and scanned the pleasure boats on Little Neck Bay. The wind from the southwest was unusually dry, as it had been all summer, and the sun had long since outstayed its welcome and become an aching presence.

A lethargy lay over the bay. Only one sail dotted the seascape: a boy in a sunfish scudding madly before the wind, playing chicken with the Savage Point dock, shooting straight for it, swerving at the last minute and capsizing. It was cocktail hour; the sun had gone over the yardarm a month or two ago, and the residents who still found peace with the hard stuff had been cocktailing in their air-conditioned dens ever since. A few speedboats tried valiantly to stir up some excitement, but the stolid cabin cruisers remained unmoving at their moorings, their backs turned.

The Mannheim boat glided slowly toward its mooring in the middle of the bay a half mile from the house. Eileen Engelhart, Fred's twenty-one-year-old daughter, sat on the prow with her sun-brown legs dangling above the water.

"She's coming in now," Engelhart said to Angel Jones, who stood just inside the deck's screened doorway.

"She must be fr-razzled," Angel said. She had won a Tallulah sound-alike contest in Minnesota forty years ago and had been speaking Bankheadese ever since.

Fred smiled, thinking that it was ridiculous that he loved this gawky creature who was almost his match in eccentricity. He glanced at her through the screening, a piebald figure in a muumuu or serape or whatever you call it that she had fashioned from a designer bedsheet. She was as inventive as he was, that was one of her attractions, creating her clothes from materials at hand, not caring that she looked like a bag lady.

As he watched, she disintegrated before his eyes. The flash blinded him, but the sight of her flying fragments was vivid in his head as the fierce compression slammed into him and sent him soaring into nowhere. Shattered eardrums never registered the roiling rumble of the explosion. He was speeding through whiteness, without pain, without any feeling at all except motion and a sense of *toward* and *away*.

Toward obliteration and away from the past. The past that he had deliberately made opaque like a shattered windshield, the remembrance of an earlier explosion and the crushing sense of guilt. Not guilt. Shame. Sadness. Shattering sadness. He had killed . . .

His body hurtled into a tree and fell to the ground, propelled prematurely to the last Shakespearean role of man, sans eyes, sans taste, sans everything. Comatose with but a secret spark in his brain still glowing in fitful defiance of his murderer—

Giesler! In the deep recess of his brain he remembered the name. He had thrown a grenade at the Gauleiter of Munich. Something happened. He had thrown it all wrong. In the scant seconds that followed he wanted to run and stop the explosion. Crazy. A grenade, like Pandora's box, once opened, couldn't be slammed shut. The explosion was a small one, nothing compared with the one that had just killed ninety-nine percent of him, but he heard it in his head all the same. The start of the shattering sadness.

He tried to say a long-forgotten act of contrition, and couldn't.

Oh, my God . . .

Across the waters of the bay the explosion was little more than a glint in the trees on the bluff, like a flower blooming and dying in a time-lapse nature movie. The low rumble that followed was lost in the wind.

Ralph Simmons didn't see it. He was sprawled in a canvas chair on Rudi Mannheim's boat, the remnant of a gin-and-tonic on the deck by his foot. He had eased out of the conversation with the other guests a half hour ago. The incessant wind, the hammering sun, and the inane blather had stupefied him. In the dullest of company he could always find something to marvel at or a person to empathize with. But today it seemed that all ten of the passengers had been withered by the summer-long drought.

Through half-closed eyes his gaze took in Rudolf Mannheim's back in the wheelhouse and, beyond him, the backs of the two young people on the prow—Eileen Engelhart with her legs dangling and her friend Teddy Thatcher on one knee beside her. Teddy was holding the tie-line in one hand, ready to tether the craft. Ralph's somewhat avuncular eyes delighted in resting on Eileen. She wore a simple black swimsuit and a flimsy white shirt over her shoulders. Unlike her homely, rawboned father, she was an exquisite miniature, scarcely over a hundred pounds, with a centerfold figure, tousled black hair, and laughing, taunting Irish eyes that must have come from her mother.

The young man, Teddy Thatcher, was another matter. He was a light-haired Englishman, good-looking yet stiff as a model in a mail-order catalogue. To Ralph he looked like he was posing now, one hand in the pocket of his lightweight jacket, demonstrating the middle-class joys of boating on Little Neck Bay. Acting as if he belonged.

Rudolf Mannheim, master of the boat, was another poser who thought he belonged. A little man standing proudly erect at the wheel, his wispy white beard blowing in the wind, he was a biblical figure waiting for God to snap his picture. Ralph found his posturing endearing.

Eileen jumped to her feet.

Teddy was crouched, tying the line to the mooring.

Ralph straightened up. Eileen was staring toward the bluff at the south end of the bay. Most of the Engelhart house was hidden from view by foliage. A billow of smoke rose where the house was supposed to be; tattered by the wind, it billowed again. Ralph idly wondered what in the world Fred Engelhart was up to.

He watched Eileen thump Teddy on the shoulder and point toward the shoreline. Teddy, still on one knee, stared up at her. She turned to Mannheim, behind the windshield. Ralph heard her this time. "The dock!" she cried. "Go to the dock!"

Mannheim nodded and smiled at her, apparently thinking she was calling him "Doc," which was how she usually addressed him. Mannheim was a psychologist with a doctorate in social work.

Eileen scrambled around the wheelhouse, hit Mannheim on the arm. "Something happened. Our house. Gotta go, gotta go." She grabbed the wheel and spun it toward shore, but the engine had been turned off.

Ralph gaped toward shore, accidentally knocking over his drink with his foot. Voices around him were saying, "What? What?" Ralph's brain was dumbly echoing the question. The incomprehensible was happening.

"Explosion," Eileen said.

Ralph tried to get out of his chair, moving his arms and legs like an overturned turtle.

He peered forward and saw that Ted was staring back at Eileen, just standing there, the boat still tethered to its mooring.

Eileen screamed, "Ted, you shithead!" She pushed Mannheim out of her way and dove over the side into the water.

Ralph called, "Wait," succeeded in getting to his feet.
A woman said, "What in God's name—?"
Someone else said, "Holy shit, the son of a bitch finally blew himself up!" Ralph recognized the voice of Judge Timmy O'Keefe.

Ralph pulled off his shirt, Bermuda shorts, and sneakers, and he bellyflopped into the water, clad only in white socks and the boxer shorts that Lillian bought him for Valentine's Day, the ones with the red hearts on them.

Lillian called, "No, Ralph," but he didn't hear her.

He surfaced, gasping as his sun-soaked body recovered from the shock of the water. He peered around looking for Eileen, didn't see her, then he saw her arm raised in the process of shucking off her flimsy white shirt. She was heading not for the dock, which was closer, but toward the far bluff on which her father had built his house.

God, that's a good half mile! The Olympics don't even have a distance that long! How can a flabby sixty-three-year-old make it? What the hell am I doing here, he wailed to himself. Wallowing in a polluted bay . . . A wave slapped him in the face, sending water up his nose and down his throat.

"Swim, damn it," he told himself. The good old sidestroke, slow and lazy, he could do it forever—or five minutes, whichever came first. He settled into a rhythm and proceeded in stately fashion through the clustered moorings. He heard voices from other boats.

"What is it?" ". . . great white shark in panties."

He concentrated on his rhythm. He couldn't see Eileen but knew she was heading for the roiling cloud of smoke on the bluff. She was undoubtedly swimming faster than he was, but someone had to stay with her, and he was doing the best he could. Why didn't her friend Teddy go with her instead of freezing up in the sudden crisis? What the hell has Fred Engelhart done to himself? The thought tugged at Ralph's insides. He swallowed some more water.

Swim. Long smooth strokes, that's the ticket. *Boop*

boop, dittum dottum, wottum choo. Stupid old song. Swim, said the momma fishie, swim if you can, and they swam and they swam all over the dam. Arms turning wooden. How come fishes and birds don't get tired? Maybe they do. Tread water. Tread air. Shit, how much farther?

His hand reached out for water and scooped mud. Bay silting up badly. Soon it'll be the Little Neck Swamp. He struggled to his feet, floundered, and fell back down. On hands and knees, he peered ahead. He was still a hundred yards from shore. Most of the Engelhart house was screened from view by foliage. As he looked, one of the interior trees burst into flames, a thing of awful beauty. The wind made the tree flare brightly, then shook its fiery ornaments free and carried them away through the air in a hailstorm of pyrotechnic pellets. *Oh, Lord God,* Ralph thought, *Fred really did blow himself up!*

His eyes found Eileen, already on shore moving toward the steps of imbedded railroad ties that led up the bluff to the house. He tried to call out to her, but his words were throttled by a tightness in his throat. She started up the steps. Since the wind was sweeping from her right to her left, none of the smoke and heat came down to block her way. What did block her was a section of roofing. Ralph saw her reach out to push it aside and recoil when it began to smolder.

Ralph stood in a foot of water and what seemed like a foot of muck. He pulled up his sagging shorts and slogged toward shore calling Eileen's name. She was scrambling to the right through marsh grass and over boulders upwind to the steps leading to the house next door.

He made his way ashore, arms and legs splayed to retain his balance, feeling like Frankenstein's monster. Eileen had disappeared, but he knew the route she had taken, and he clumsily followed it to the stone steps in the neighbor's sea wall.

He paused. What the hell was the name of these people? Even though they lived just down the street from him and they had exchanged waves and hellos countless times, the name eluded him. No matter. He labored up the steps in socks now filthy with tidal mud. He found himself on a plush lawn, which obviously had been watered regularly despite the city's ban. To his left a deep thicket of bushes and stunted trees defined the border between this property and Engelhart's.

A skimpily clad woman stood on the lawn, a forgotten cocktail glass in her hand, transfixed by the turmoil of smoke and fire beyond the bordering growth. There were tricklets of blood on her face. Behind her the windows on that side of the house were shattered. A middle-aged man in baggy shorts was watering the house with a hose—senselessly, since the wind was blowing the fire away from him.

Ralph waved at them weakly, and lumbered toward the thicket, saw no obvious opening that Eileen might have made ahead of him. He gritted his teeth and plunged through, flailing with his arms, unheeding of the brambles that tore at his pale flesh.

He broke through to open ground and stopped. "Oh, Jesus," he breathed. The great eccentric house, Fred's pride and joy! The far side of it was still standing, ripped open by the blast, a bedroom exposed— Eileen's, if he remembered correctly—dense smoke coming from her bed. The nearer portion of the house was a scattered pile of cement chunks and blazing rubble. Fred couldn't possibly—he was too alive, too feisty—

Ralph raised his arms to shield himself from the heat and the awful glare.

Eileen was to his right, momentarily halted in the act of reaching down to something on the ground below a tree. Particles swirled around her like a swarm of fiery gnats. As he looked, the strength seemed to drain out of her, and she started to slump.

He caught her before she hit the ground, held her up. His arms were quivering, his breath rasping.

Then they were sitting on the ground. He was patting her shoulder, unable to say anything. He peered beyond her to the strangely angled heap of flesh and bones on the ground—the remains of Fred Engelhart, his red hair tousled, his homely face unmarked. His eyes were open, looking up at the tree that had stopped his flight.

"I wanted to close his eyes to keep them from getting burned," she said in a dull voice. "And I couldn't."

"'Sokay," Ralph muttered. "Jus' gotta rest a moment." He fought off the lethargy and stood up.

She said, "Shouldn't we—?"

"Do what?" He pulled her to her feet. "Can't move him. Gotta get ambulance. Come on."

She looked down at her father. "Is he—dead?"

"Maybe not." He knew Fred was dead. He looked around. The dead-end street on which the house was situated was blocked by the blazing debris. The wind was whipping the fire up and away from them in a maelstrom of smoke and fiery particles, but the heat radiating back toward them was intense.

They pushed their way back through the thicket. The woman had dropped her cocktail glass and was kneeling on the grass. The man was mindlessly watering his house.

Ralph called, "Where's the phone?"

The man waved vaguely toward the house.

Ralph found a wall phone in the kitchen. From memory he punched out the number of the volunteer ambulance corps and directed the dispatcher to send the ambulance to the house he was in rather than the dead-end lane that was blocked by the fire. Only then did he call 911, but he hung up when he heard the fire sirens in the distance. Someone else had apparently given the alarm.

He gazed wearily at Eileen, saw a shudder go through her.

"Hang on, honey," he said, squeezing her shoulder. "He's safe where he is. The fire won't backtrack on him."

She lowered her head and shook it.

He became aware of his ludicrous state of undress.

"Gotta get some clothes on," he mumbled. "Be right back." His own house was only two minutes away.

He plodded to the kitchen door.

"Uncle Ralph?"

He turned.

"Does this have something to do with the white rose?"

The white rose? He had forgotten all about that. What a strange question. He shrugged wearily. "Stay right here, I'll only be a minute," he said.

He went out the door.

But Eileen Engelhart didn't stay right there. She went back through the thicket and crouched over her father's broken body to shelter it from the swirling particles. The volunteer ambulance workers and the city firemen came on her at the same time from different directions. They marveled that she had only minor burns.

2.

Ralph Simmons was one of the few outsiders who had seen the white rose. It was a week before the explosion. Penelope Potter later claimed she had seen it, but her sighting was in the form of a vision, which couldn't be verified objectively.

Ralph was a former newspaper executive who had been forced into early retirement shortly before his beloved *New York Herald-Courier* itself expired from fiscal anemia, for which Ralph was blamed. He had been unable to stop the flow of advertising dollars to television. His first wife Margaret had also been slowly withering away at the time from cancer, and Ralph had taken refuge in the bottle for several years until he was pulled from the brink of cirrhosis by his former secretary Lillian Caplin. They made an endearingly chubby couple, and anyone who chanced to observe them cavorting in the privacy of their shower would be reminded of pink hippopotamuses out of Disney.

Ralph's exercise of choice was walking, and when Fred Engelhart arrived in Savage Point to build his house, it was only natural for Ralph to include Schmidt's Lane in his daily itinerary.

He was fascinated by the wild-haired man who was bossing the erection of an eccentric house. He had the impression that the man was making it up on a day-today basis, continually changing the original plans—to curve a deck around a tree, for example, or lower the level of a room to conform to the contours of the bluff—so that the final cost of construction must have been truly fierce.

The flooring of the first street level was being hammered into place, and the elongated man with the reddish-gray mop of hair was darting about making chalk marks and instructing the carpenters. Ralph was standing below them in the lane, watching.

Engelhart called down to him, "Any suggestions?" Sarcastically.

Ralph said, "Just wondering if you can use a drink."

"What time is it?"

"What difference does that make?" Ralph said.

Engelhart's knobby face broke into a grin. "That's the correct answer, sir! Hold on a minute."

After further advising the carpenters, he joined Ralph in the lane. Ralph told him that the welcome wagon was his house on Dover, the next street down.

As they walked, Fred said, "What's with the people around here? They act like they're mad at me."

"You frighten them," Ralph said. "You're changing things, and they don't like changes."

The Simmons wood-frame house was old, unlovely in design, and in need of paint. The large lawn was as brown and bristly as an old-fashioned doormat. Engelhart nodded approvingly. "I see you're not concerned with appearances, keeping up with the Joneses—"

"It's not that, Fred. Just that I'm on a penny-pinching pension, and I have to practice triage on my repairs. On top of that, I'm lazy as hell—"

Ralph led him through the house to the back porch with the rusted screening. At that first meeting Lillian seemed to be cowed by the gangling, high-energy stranger, and she retreated to the kitchen.

The two men talked easily over gin-and-tonics on that day and on many days after that, and they discovered that, despite their antithetical appearance and deportment, they were kindred spirits. Each had a disrespect for conformity, a contempt for social pretensions, and an enormous curiosity about everything and everyone on the planet.

Ralph mentioned the similarity to Lillian, and she said, "Does that make you a genius too?"

He lowered his eyes. "That's not for me to say."

"Me neither," she said.

Ralph thought that was funny, whether she intended it to be or not.

Over the months Fred Engelhart's house succeeded in being built despite his supervision, and the good people of Savage Point thought it was an elaborate practical joke on them. *Split-level* was the word for it, with at least nine distinct levels from the concrete workroom in the basement up the bluff through rooms stacked haphazardly like children's blocks to what he called his "bell tower," though it wasn't a tower and had no bell. It was a glass-enclosed top deck perched among treetops looking north over Little Neck Bay to the open waters of Long Island Sound and beyond to the rust-colored complex of Co-op City in the Bronx.

A week before the explosion Ralph and Lillian were in the bell tower with Engelhart and Angel having end-of-day drinks. The wind was buffeting the trees, and Fred Engelhart was moving about restlessly. The motions gave Ralph a moment of dizziness.

"Sit down, Fred," he growled, "before I throw up on your shoes."

"A vomitorium, of course!" Engelhart exclaimed. "I should have included a vomitorium! The jet set of old Rome had one in every house . . ."

Ralph said, "Fred, please," and Engelhart sat down.

Angel Jones let out a throaty laugh. "Speaking of such delicate matters, while the house was going up the dreary old crab next door kept hollering at Fred about one thing or another day after day, hollering and complaining and bitching until Fred told him the new house wasn't going to have a cesspool. He pointed to a spot right on the property line and said that was where he was going to put his outhouse if the gentleman didn't keep his peace."

"A three-seater," Fred said. "With a crescent moon cut in the door."

"Of course, they didn't have privies in Germany when Fred was a boy," Angel said. "He didn't know about them until I gave him an old book by a man named Chic Sales. I think they appealed to Fred's architectural instincts."

"So what happened with the guy next door?" Lillian asked.

"Hasn't said a word to Fred since, has he, Fred?"

"Just stands there and glares. I tried making friends with him, but—he seems to enjoy being an enemy."

The conversation meandered and, at length, veered to the local garden club, a dull subject if ever there was one. But Engelhart took it as a signal to jump to his feet and start down the staircase, saying, "There's something I want to show you two experts."

Ralph looked questioningly at Lillian. He was aware that the sun was setting and the cocktail hour was about over. To him it had been a happy Happy Hour even though he had sensed the extra tension in the host.

Angel said, "I believe he's gone to get the flower. We were both quite mystified."

Lillian said, "If he thinks we know anything about flowers—"

Fred Engelhart was back in the room holding a white box out to Ralph. "This came in the mail this morning. Maybe you can make some sense out of it."

Resting in the box on red tissue paper was a large white rose, past full bloom and starting to wither. A hatpin with an opalescent head was thrust through the center of the flower pinning a scrap of red ribbon to its heart. It looked as if the flower was bleeding.

Ralph said, "If you're asking me, I'd say it's a rose."

"Definitely a rose," Lillian said. "Just like the one that Ken and Barbie gave Ralph when we celebrated Ralph's birthday at the club. Remember, Ralph?"

Angel said, "Ken and Barbie?"

"Oh, you know them," Lillian said. "I always think of them as the two dolls, they're so good-looking and so nice it makes you sick. I mean they seem so—fake."

"She's talking about Don and Betsy Grant," Ralph said. "They're really a very pleasant couple."

"Perfect, that's the trouble," Lillian said.

"It was damn embarrassing. Bigmouth here told everybody in the dining room it was my birthday, and Don disappeared for a few minutes and came back with this big rose, it was a pink one—"

"Pale pink. Very pale."

"And he tried to pin it on my jacket. Then the whole damn room—"

Angel interrupted him. "We don't think this one's so innocent. We think the intent is malicious. You can just feel the evil in it. Br-r-r."

Fred peered intently at Ralph. "What does it remind you of?" he asked.

"Pin the tail on the donkey," Ralph said. "No, it looks like some jolly soul drew blood from the rose. Is there some dumb message here? Blood from a turnip and all that?"

Fred was nodding somberly. "Voodoo," he said. "Incantation. Needle in the doll's gizzard. *Auf Wiedersehen*, farewell, Fred Engelhart."

"Aw, come on," Ralph said. "This is a flower, not a doll. How's your gizzard? Any shooting pains? Someone sent you a flower, that's all. And it came from—" He looked at the top of the box. "—Amy's Flower Boutique. I know the place. Wasn't there a card? There's generally a card."

Fred grimaced. "Just my name on it, that's all."

After a moment, Ralph said, "May I see it?"

Fred Engelhart held out a small white oblong. Printed on it in block letters was one word: "Friedrich."

Ralph said, "What's with this *Friedrich* bit? You're just plain Fred, aren't you? Not Frederick or Fred anything else. Just Fred."

"Right, but I was christened Friedrich. I haven't used

it for forty years. It sounded so alien when I came here."

"And that's your shameful secret!" Ralph said. "So what does the flower mean?"

Engelhart moved his shoulders as if shrugging off a coat or something unpleasant. "Could be a promotional gimmick to sell canned goods, couldn't it?"

"No," Ralph said.

"Then I don't know what it means. Who's ready for another drink?"

"It goes back to something in Germany, doesn't it?" Ralph said.

Lillian said, "Lay off, Ralph. If he doesn't want to talk about it—"

"It isn't that, Lillian," Engelhart said. He sat down on the edge of his chair. "Yes, it is. The white rose and the name Friedrich. The red could be blood, and the pin could be death. It could be saying it's my turn to die. But it can't be. The only one who knows about it is Rudi Mannheim, and he wouldn't do a thing like this. He's too—too—"

"Dumb?" Angel Jones suggested.

Engelhart grunted. "No, Rudi isn't dumb. He's unimaginative. Plodding. Typically Germanic, but—"

Angel said, "Anti-Nazi, dar-rling."

Lillian scowled and turned to her host. "Forget about it, Fred. The pin is for putting it on your lapel. Someone wants to give you a nice boutonniere, that's all."

Engelhart half smiled. "If you say so, Lilly."

A few minutes later Ralph and Lillian rose to leave, just as Eileen swept in with her English boyfriend, Ted Thatcher. They had been to a movie in Bayside, a blood-spurting chiller. Amid the greetings and Eileen's funny description of some of the more revolting scenes, Angel pulled Ralph aside.

Ralph grinned at her, as he always did when he contemplated the theatrically shabby woman. He embraced her bony shoulder and said, "Alone at last."

She said, "Do you know that Shirer book on Nazi Germany?"

"By heart," Ralph said, still grinning.

"Look up 'White Rose.' It's only a guess, but look it up."

Ralph started to ask a question, but Eileen had come over to hug him, and Lillian said, "Here now, that's enough of that," and Ralph said, "No, it isn't. Come back here, you minx," and Eileen grinned wickedly and turned away. Lillian said, "Minx?"

Young Ted Thatcher was standing awkwardly beside Fred, neither of them speaking, Fred still holding the flower box. Ralph tried to think back to the time when he was an awkward twenty-one-year-old (like Ted) unable to make small talk with the parents of the girl he was dating, suddenly recalling that when he was twenty-one he wasn't a trembling swain but a quivering zombie on Omaha Beach hiding from death, blindly doing what the lieutenant told him to do, somehow remaining alive from moment to moment, faintly surprised that this was so.

Ralph shook his head. What brought that on, for God's sake?

He said to Lillian, "Come on, honey, let's blow this joint."

He took the flower box from Fred. "I'll check with Amy tomorrow and find out who sent it," he said.

Fred Engelhart nodded passively. Which was uncharacteristic of this lively man.

Amy Kaltenborn leaned on the stack of tissue paper on her counter and said to Ralph, "It's painful to see a flower murdered like that, even an inferior breed. It's not the sort of flower a florist would carry. Too fragile, short-lived, undernourished. But there must be a hundred rose bushes in Savage Point with flowers like that. One of your neighbors must have sent it and used our box. If you find out who, let me know. I feel I've been slandered."

He said, "Maybe you should have an ASPCF." Amy looked puzzled, so he added, "To stop cruelty to flowers."

"Good idea," she said.

Back home, Ralph couldn't find his copy of *The Rise and Fall of The Third Reich*.

He said to Lillian, "Well, I tried."

3.

The first alarm after the explosion came into Engine Company 114, based on a side street near Northern Boulevard. It was the old folks' home of the New York Fire Department, the depository for burnt-out cases. Most of their calls were kitchen fires, brush fires, and false alarms. Working fires were scarce, and when they did occur, second and third alarms brought in other companies to help. Arson was almost unheard of.

When the call came in that afternoon in late August, Captain Tom Noonan had the engine rolling within fifteen seconds. Not bad. The unspoken prayer came reflexively from long practice: *Dear God, don't let anyone get hurt.* Danny Ferrara, the only young firefighter in the company, was driving; he was a provo assigned to Noonan, the old-timer, for proper breaking in; a hyperactive kid gung-ho to wage war on real, honest-to-God conflagrations where whole families are trapped and he, Ferrara, plunges in and saves them along with their pet dogs, Fluffy and Duke. Not these piddling fires that a couple of teenagers could put out by pissing on them. Ferrara was a real pain in the ass to Noonan, but Noonan loved him with a special affection because he reminded him of himself twenty-five years earlier, when Noonan was getting his baptism by fire in

Bed-Stuy. Ferrara was already a good nozzle man, a little too impetuous maybe, but he had yet to learn the respect for the power of fire that only comes from experience—if you survive.

The engine thundered up Savage Point Road toward the point, siren wailing. Topping the overpass over the Port Washington line, Noonan peered ahead. All he could see were trees, some of which were already showing fall colors more than a month ahead of time. "Hope it's just a kitchen," he said.

"Yeah, sure," Ferrara said.

They wheeled down the northern side of the overpass, dull green and autumn-colored trees blocking their view. It wasn't until they came to Dover Street that they could see through the trees, and Noonan said, "Holy shit, we got ourselves a freakin' forest fire!"

The fire was still confined to Schmidt's Lane. The Engelhart site was hidden by dense smoke. The house next to it was blazing, and the roof of the brick house on the corner was smoking. But the sight that made Noonan grab for the mike and call for an all-borough alarm was the trees that were blazing fiercely in the wind, creating an updraft, getting stronger with each passing moment, that shot the roiling gray smoke high in the air, funneled by the prevailing southwest wind, however, in a northeasterly direction across the breadth of Savage Point, the whole effusion electrified not by lightning but thousands of fiery particles dancing in a thermodynamic frenzy.

Noonan sat in the cab gripped by a sense of helplessness he had never felt before in the face of a fire. This was a monster that mere man could never control.

Ferrara and the others, well trained by Noonan, were pulling hose, linking the inch-and-a-half sections, attaching the engine to a hydrant a hundred feet from Schmidt's Lane.

"The second house, Cappy?" Ferrara called.

"No, the brick one."

"It's not on fire!"

"It will be."

Ferrara and another man ran the empty line to the house. He waved, and the line was charged with water. He and his backup wrestled with the now-living, anacondalike hose and shot the great stream at the smoking roof just as the whole roof burst into flame.

"Take it," Ferrara said to the backup. "I'm going in."

The house faced on Savage Point Road. Ferrara ran awkwardly in his big boots to the front door.

Noonan roared, "Come back here, you damn fool!"

Ferrara whirled and stamped his feet like a petulant child. "But somebody may be in there!"

Noonan, who had lumbered to the intersection out of the direct path of the fire, still felt the heated air singing the hair on the back of his neck. "Come here, Danny," he said, beckoning.

The young man raced back, his face red from the heat, his eyes blazing with anger. "But—but—"

"You're not going anywhere without an airpack," Noonan said coldly. He had to raise his voice over the increasing roar.

As they faced each other the first ladder company arrived from Little Neck, and men were leaping from the truck, already masked, carrying axes and halligans.

"You gave up the nozzle," Noonan said to Ferrra. "That's a criminal offense in my eyes. Now get over there and take it back. We'll talk later."

Noonan watched him retake his position at the hose. Maybe he learned something, Noonan thought, maybe he didn't.

Suddenly a great beech tree on the east side of Savage Point Road, across from Schmidt's Lane, burst into flames. Noonan groaned and ran back to the cab of his engine.

"The fire's out of control," he told headquarters. "There are maybe a hundred houses in its path, and there's no way we can stop it. Water pressure's dropping, every damn fool in the point is probably watering his house. Find out how long it would take a fireboat to get here, though I don't know if it can get close enough to shore to do any good. What we have here is a forest fire building into a firestorm. We need hoses and more hoses and a lot of heavy prayin'."

The truck company's rescue squad came out of the brick house, which showed fire in the upstairs windows, and reported that the house was empty.

"Good," Noonan said. "Now let's hope that every other soul on this damned peninsula has gone to Canada for the weekend. Pray for a miracle, Danny."

The only miracle was finding Eileen Engelhart alive, crouched over the broken body of her father. With Danny and his backup covering them with water, the rescue squad made their way down Schmidt's Lane along the southern periphery of the fire, evacuating residents who hadn't already fled from the two houses on that side of the lane. At the end they came on the pitiful tableau just as the volunteer crew, led by Ralph Simmons, broke through the thicket on the far side. In less than a minute the firemen cleared a path through the foliage for the volunteers to take off the first two casualties.

It was Danny who spotted the blackened figure in the side yard of the blazing house next to Engelhart's. He covered it with the hose while the rescue squad ran in a crouch to drag it from the scene. One of the rescuers with a faulty airpack had to be rescued as well.

Other fire companies arrived along with the battalion chief. Noonan suggested that they be set up on Center and East Drives in the path of the fire to fight it head on, although Noonan knew it was a hopeless mission. Unless the wind changed, this monster was going to march inexorably across the peninsula until it reached Harper's Cove.

More battalion chiefs arrived and took command, leaving Noonan and Engine Company 114 where they were, throwing water on a conflagration that paid them no mind but went its voracious way consuming everything in its path. To Danny Ferrara it was a fire god calling devotees to come and throw themselves into its embrace. For a fleeting moment he felt the lure, became enraged at the loony thought and, cursing wildly, continued to play his trickle of water on the flank of the monster.

Lillian Simmons emerged slowly from her initial befuddlement. First there was Eileen Englehart going off her rocker and plunging off the side of the boat, then Ralph throwing off his clothes and following her into the water. What did he think he was doing? Bobbing up and down with an antique sidestroke that made him look like he was treading water with an anchor tied to one leg. "Come back, you crazy nut!" she called.

Clutching his Bermuda shorts, shirt, and sneakers in one arm, she pressed the other fist to her chest to slow the thumping of her heart. Lillian was a faded blonde with an oval face and what they call a maternal figure, meaning she was about twenty-five pounds overweight, much of it in her bust, tummy, and butt built up over the years by a ravening addiction to chocolate. She muttered, "Oh, my God," with each breath she let out.

Rudi Mannheim was frantically squawking his air horn and shouting for the launch, his thin voice lost in the wind. Young Ted Thatcher emerged from his own private funk, untied the mooring line, and called to Mannheim to follow Eileen and Ralph to the far shore. Mannheim said, "No, no, no, no," shaking his head.

Lillian grabbed his arm. "Why not?"

"Twenty-five thousand reasons, Lillian," he said. "That's what this craft cost. We'd be caught on the mudflats before we were halfway there."

Mannheim's wife Prudence said quietly, "The launch will be quicker," then added, "if it ever gets here."

Lillian never did understand Prudence, attributing the failure of communication to Prudence's Quaker background. Who, for instance, would go sailing on the sound in the middle of a scorching summer dressed in a full-length, grayish print dress with a full slip and

God knows what else underneath? Yet somehow she was the appropriate complement to the Germanic pomposity of her social-worker husband.

Lillian dismissed the two other couples on the boat—a drunken civil court judge and his excessively polite wife, and a mannish architect and her mousy husband. Judge O'Keefe said, "He's a month and a half late. Shoulda happened on the Fourth of July, don't y'think?" The mousy husband said, "You're right, Judge." His wife said, "I truly believe the ghost of Ayn Rand came back and blew up Fred's house. It was an insult to architecture." The judge said, "Yeah, a ghost did it," and he laughed.

Lillian saw Eileen stagger ashore beneath what seemed to be a boiling fire. Ralph was slogging through two feet of water far from shore. She saw him fall, get up, and stagger on. She prayed that Fred and Angel weren't there. The launch was finally approaching the boat.

Lillian said, "Judge."

O'Keefe beamed at her. "Call me Timmy, Lillian. My friends call me Timmy."

She said, "Judge, you stink."

He looked as if he had been slapped. "What brought that on?"

She said to Mannheim, "How can you put up with these empty-headed bigots?"

Mannheim grimaced painfully. Prudence said, "Please, they're our guests . . . Ah, here's our transportation."

The judge was saying, "Did I do something wrong?" and his wife was soothing him, saying, "You have to understand, Timmy, she's a *friend* of Mr. Engelhart. Let's go, dear."

With one arm hugging Ralph's clothing, Lillian eyed the open launch being held against the Mannheim boat by the young man who piloted it. Agility was never one of her strong points, and she mistrusted her ability to transfer her round little body to the swaying launch without falling. Ted Thatcher had leaped easily and was glaring at the distant shore where fire glinted through the turbulent smoke. The judge lost his balance and fell on his behind.

Lillian said, "Ted!" sharply, holding out her free hand. The young man jumped, then gallantly helped her make the transfer.

He was in a great state of agitation. She could see that. His handsome face was pinched with stress, and for the first time in the year that she had known him she felt sympathy. Until now he had just been the pleasant stranger who had moved into the house next door with his mother and who had soon become the steady boyfriend of Eileen. The very things that attracted Eileen—his "differentness" from American boys, his "classy" accent, his well-groomed good looks, his polite attentiveness, his "civilized" laugh, his air of mystery, his poise, mostly his unfailing poise—all tended to keep warm-hearted Lillian at arm's length. Now the unnatural poise was breached, and he was showing emotion.

"I should have gone with her," he muttered. "I just stood there like a blasted mummy."

You mean dummy, Lillian thought, but she said, "You were surprised, Ted. Everyone was surprised. You can't blame yourself for that."

As they putt-putted slowly to the dock, he stood tensed, watching the fire's progress. His hands were hidden in the pockets of his flimsy jacket, but she bet they were clenched.

When they disembarked onto the float at the base of the dock, Ted raced up the ramp and disappeared. Lillian was the last off the launch. She dropped one of Ralph's sneakers and had to pick it up. The judge made it up the ramp with the help of his wife. The architect dragged her husband up, saying, "Our house! It may hit our house!" No one paid attention to Lillian. Even Rudolf Mannheim, ordinarily the perfect host, was concerned about his own house, which was on Shore Road two blocks to the north.

Lillian hustled along the dock to the shore. There was Ralph's little red Skyhawk parked nose-in to the curb. The keys were in the Bermuda shorts she was carrying, but they wouldn't do her any good. She had never learned to drive.

She took a tighter grip on the bundle of clothes and started walking—south toward the fire, hidden behind the abundance of trees, smoke billowing above them. Her breathing was becoming painful. There didn't seem to be any air. Perspiration stung her eyes. Gravel had gotten into her thin sandals and was stabbing her feet. Looking ahead to where Shore Road turned inland toward Savage Point Road, she saw Eric Bushman running around the corner of his house with a garden hose in his hand. He was a tall, well-preserved, elderly man, skeleton-thin, perpetually bent forward as if walking into a stiff breeze. He reminded Lillian of a praying mantis.

As she approached, the stream of water from his hose visibly slackened and fell short of the roof. He held the nozzle high over his head as if to stretch the water itself.

Lillian halted in the road, attempting to catch her breath. Bushman was tugging at the hose with frenzied motions that were quite uncharacteristic of a man who had had a distinguished career in the country's foreign service. He turned to glare at the roar of the still unseen fire.

Lillian called to him.

It took him a full second to recognize her, then he said, "Who would have thought that a little explosion would set off something like this? It's illogical. And now there's no water!"

Three steps led up from the road to the path to his large house. Lillian put Ralph's clothing on the top step. "I'm done in," she said. "Can I leave these here?"

"If you don't mind getting them burned," Bushman said. He shook the limp hose. "This is outrageous."

"Thanks," Lillian said, and went on toward the fire. Her thoughts were jumbled. Foreign service people were supposed to keep their cool. Oh, well. It was only natural for people to get panicky if their house was in the path of a fire.

At the corner of Savage Point Road she turned south, rounded a turn in the road, and stopped short. Directly ahead was a scene out of hell, fire raging on both sides of the road—and *high*! Tall trees were blazing. The road was blocked not only by the fire but a phalanx of fire engines on the far side. She didn't know how long she gaped before she could marshal her thoughts. She had to get around this and get to Ralph. He needed her, she knew it.

She retraced her steps to the next corner, Albemarle Road, an uphill street. People were moving about aimlessly, shocked, giving voice to the turmoil within themselves. Lillian ignored them because she couldn't speak. Halfway up the street she was sobbing.

She turned right on Center Drive. Large amount of windblown smoke here but no fire. Yet. Firemen were watering the houses. Judith, the architect, and her mousy husband were standing on the sidewalk across the street from their modern house. Judith was calling instructions to the firemen, who were paying no attention to her.

Lillian plunged through the smoke, sobbing, gasping. She muttered, "Sorry," to the couple, and plodded on. Since thinking of the destruction of Fred's house was too painful, her mind returned to Ted Thatcher. So the young man was a real person, after all. He had shown a vulnerability she had never seen before. Yes, he should have gone with Eileen. Should-haves are awful things. The guilt associated with them can be blown all out of proportion and become devastating.

Even so, Ted Thatcher was still an enigma to her. Handsome people dazzle, she thought; the surface is so bright you can't see the configurations behind it. Not his fault, really. And yet—there was something his mother had said that strange Thanksgiving Day last fall. About Teddy, as she called him. The recollection eluded her.

She threaded her way through the hoses on Center

Drive. A fireman said roughly, "You're not supposed to be here, lady."

She glared at him speechlessly. Angry retorts formed in her mind. All that came out was, "Go fight a fire, damn it!" And that was when she was well past him.

What was that elusive thing about Teddy? . . .

4.

Less than a year before the firestorm. The man who had owned the house next door to the Simmonses had been an eccentric millionaire who had turned his backyard into a miniature golf course with fiendishly difficult holes to negotiate. When he died rather abruptly, his family put the house on the market, and it was purchased by a middle-aged woman and her twenty-year-old son at the height of the real-estate boom. They paid eight hundred thousand dollars for it, and Ralph concluded they were loaded.

Ralph pulled his "welcome wagon" stunt, and he came back dragging his figurative wagon behind him. "She said it was sweet of us to think of them," he reported to Lillian, "but she was teddibly busy, don't you know, and could we please put off our invitation for a fortnit."

"Come on. She didn't really say 'fortnit,' did she?"

"No," Ralph admitted. "What she was really saying behind her British accent was 'Bug off, you toad.'"

It was early fall, and Ralph and Lillian still spent a good part of their time on their screened-in back porch. They watched, appalled, as workmen brutally destroyed the miniature golf course. Their dismay was somewhat assuaged when they saw a large swimming pool installed in its stead. Ralph renewed his welcoming invitation and again was told veddy politely to bug off.

The day after the new neighbors filled the pool with water the son went back to college, the weather turned cold, and the pool lay there unused, gathering leaves. "I bet she stocked it with piranha," Ralph growled. And Lillian said, "You have a bad case of sour grapes, Ralph. Take an Alka-Seltzer and forget it."

On Thanksgiving Day the whole Northeast was blessed with one of the loveliest Indian summers in memory. Lillian had planned to have her daughter and her small family come down from Westchester for the holiday feast, but at the last minute one of the grandchildren came down instead with the mumps, and the family had to stay home. So Ralph and Lillian invited Fred Engelhart, his daughter Eileen, and Angel Jones instead.

Ralph apologized for the last-minute invitation, but Engelhart assured him they had only planned to eat at the club and that Ralph and Lillian had saved them from that cold celebration.

After dinner the two men were shooed out of the kitchen, and they strolled in the backyard holding brandy glasses, smoking cigars and basking in the warm breeze. Neither of them were regular cigar smokers, but Ralph the American told the German-born Fred that brandy and a postfeast cigar were part of the ritual handed down by the Indians.

Then Ralph related the story of his previous neighbor's demise. The man had indeed died abruptly, he had been murdered, decapitated as a matter of fact, and the headless corpse had been thrown on Ralph's mulch pile. Ralph pointed to the pile behind some straggly bushes.

Fred Engelhart glanced from the pile to the large, rambling house next door, which he could see through the many gaps in the privet hedge separating the properties. "It's an ill-starred house," he said. "Your friend Black has to be roaming through it looking for his head."

Ralph laughed at the image that Engelhart had raised. "If you're right, poor Dave has to have been frightened off by the English witch who lives there now."

"Is that her?" Fred asked.

Ralph followed his friend's gaze.

The woman stood alongside the pool, her trim figure sheathed in an elegant black cocktail dress, a flower pinned over her collarbone rather like a high-school kid's corsage. Her auburn hair, pulled back into a bun, glittered with some sort of spangles. Even from a distance Ralph could see that her large eyes were made to dominate her face by the dark makeup that outlined them. He was surprised to see that she was a strikingly handsome woman.

"All dressed up and no place to go," he muttered.

Fred remained silent, and Ralph glanced at him. Fred was staring. The woman was returning the stare. Ralph started to hum "Some Enchanted Evening." He got to "across a crowded hedge," when he noticed the strange look on Fred's face. The look faded as he watched, an uneasy memory flickering off.

"I'd introduce you," Ralph said. "But I'm afraid you'd get frostbitten."

"I don't want to meet her," Engelhart said. He started toward the back porch.

The woman called, "I say, hello there." She moved toward the dividing hedge. Her manner was unexpectedly friendly. "Is the welcome wagon still in operation, Mr. Simmons?"

After a stunned moment, Ralph said, "Like that girly show in Piccadilly, we never close. Come on over."

Suddenly her son was with her, and Ralph greeted them at the gap in the hedge. "I suppose we should fill out this old hedge," he said. "Good hedges make good neighbors."

"Rubbish," the woman said, stepping regally through the opening. "Going through one's front door is so formal we'd seldom do it. This is much chummier."

"Welcome to the Simmons backyard, celebrated in song and story. Call me Ralph."

She laughed pleasantly. "And you call me Marlene. Isn't this delightfully rustic? This is my son Teddy. He's home from college for the long weekend."

Ralph clasped the young man's hand. "Good to know you, Teddy. What college is that?" He wondered if the name was Terry and only sounded like Teddy coming from her.

"The University of Virginia, sir." He bent stiffly from the waist. Nothing informal about this young squirt, Ralph thought, noting the semiformal attire of white turtleneck and blue blazer with some sort of golden crest embroidered on the breast pocket.

Ralph turned to introduce Fred Engelhart, but he wasn't there. "So, come on in," he said. "We were just having a spot of brandy. Will that do?" He wondered what had come over him. He had never said "spot of brandy" in his life.

"That will do perfectly," she said.

He led them onto the back porch with the rusted screening, where he dumped his cigar on an ashtray, and then into the living room. "It isn't much," he started to say fatuously, "but—"

Eileen Engelhart was on the sofa watching a football game on television. "I got kicked out of the kitchen too, Uncle Ralph," she said, sitting up straight.

Ralph introduced them. "It's Thatcher, isn't it? Marlene, this is Eileen Engelhart, Fred Engelhart's daughter."

Teddy moved to get a better look at the TV screen. "Who's playing?" he asked Eileen.

"Lions and Vikings. Zip, zip. Neither one of them's any good."

"Virginia never has a good team," Teddy said.

His mother said to Ralph, "Fred Engelhart? Is he the gentleman who was in the backyard just now?"

"The very same. Hey, Lil," he called. "We got company.... Now for a splash of Hennessey to properly welcome the Thatchers to the quaint but pretentious community of Savage Point." He moved to the breakfront that served as his dry bar.

Lillian came out of the kitchen, beaming, wiping her

hands on a towel. "Wow, don't you look spiffy!" she said to Marlene. She wore an apron that said: LIL'S CATERING SERVICE.

She was followed by Angel Jones, who always appeared to be slipcovered rather than dressed. After being introduced, Angel said, "I'm Fred's leading lady, you might say. Have you ever trod the boards, Mrs. Thatcher?"

"Great heavens, no," Marlene said with a tinkling laugh. "Whatever gave you that thought?"

"I can tell when a person's on stage," Angel said. "You'd have made a great actress."

"How sweet of you to say that." Marlene smiled.

Ralph hastened to bring the lady her drink. "Happy Thanksgiving Day, ma'am. May the Thatchers prosper, and may the wind always be at your back."

Lillian said, "You're mixing your toasts, Ralph."

The son was sitting beside Eileen on the sofa, looking at the football game. Eileen was looking at him. Ralph asked him what he would like to drink, and Teddy said, "Oh, anything. I'm not really a drinker. A little port, perhaps."

"No have got," Ralph said. "How about Campari with a squirt of seltzer? That's what Eileen drinks."

"Then that's what I would like too," said the young man.

Ralph suddenly became aware that Engelhart was missing. "Where's Fred?" he asked.

"He had to go home," Angel said. "Something about an experiment with sand he's conducting. Ordinary Jones-Beach-type sand. Can you imagine a grown man playing with sand?"

The living room was small, and the crowd noise coming from the TV was intrusive, and Ralph suggested they all adjourn to the back porch. Eileen and Teddy elected to stay where they were.

The conversation on the back porch was halting. Ralph blurted out how sorry he and Lillian had been to see the miniature golf course go, adding quickly that replacing it with a swimming pool was a grand idea.

"Yes," Marlene said. "It's for Teddy. He's on the swimming team at Virginia. He's really a top-notch swimmer. So was his father until his asthma slowed him and he put on weight. Bucky was a dear, dear man who really missed his swimming in later years."

"Bucky was your husband?"

"Yes, he had a ridiculous name. Old, old family. Donald Buckminster Thatcher. He insisted that everyone call him Bucky. He wanted to be one of the regular fellows."

"What did he do for a living?"

Marlene laughed lightly. "Not much of anything, I'm afraid. He fancied himself an inventor, rather like your friend Mr. Engelhart. He loved to tinker in his workshop until the arthritis stilled his fingers, poor man. That's when he took to drink. It was his only consolation."

"I know how he felt," Ralph said, remembering his own dependency on booze after his first wife died. "Did you come from the same sort of background? I mean, old family, money?"

"No, the money was all on his side. I'm interested in your Mr. Engelhart. I've heard of him, of course. He must be a fascinating man in person. Spouting new ideas all the time, like that geyser in your Yellowstone Park."

"Old Faithful," Lillian said.

"Is he like that?" Marlene asked.

Ralph and Lillian looked to Angel Jones, who said, "It's not all fun and games, but I can say this. There's never a dull moment when he's around."

"You mention background, Ralph," Marlene said. "What's his? Was he born in Menlo Park like Mr. Edison?"

Ralph grinned. "Not exactly. He was born and raised in Germany, that's all I know. He came here after the war." Ralph turned to Angel. "Do you know any more about him than that, Angel?"

"Not really," Angel said. "He never speaks of his childhood. When he came here he married a girl of Irish extraction named Mary Monahan, of all things. I don't know anything about her except that she died. Of what, I don't know, but she must have been quite young. So Fred has had to be mother and father to Eileen. He's not the motherly type, I'm afraid."

"I find that extremely interesting," Marlene said. "Mr. Engelhart and I have something in common. Teddy was only five when Bucky died in the fire. So I, too, had to be mother and father to my child. Isn't that a coincidence."

Lillian said, "I'm sure you've done a wonderful job! He's such an attractive young man! And such manners!"

Ralph said, "Your husband died in a fire?"

Marlene raised her drink to her lips. "I always think of this as brandy in a bubble," she said, trying to giggle girlishly. "It gives one a sense of luxury, don't you think? Delicious wickedness." She shivered delicately.

Ralph knew he was again being told to bug off, but he decided to be obtuse. "It's always a tragedy when a young father dies so suddenly," he said.

Marlene Thatcher raised her large eyes to his. "It wasn't really so sudden. Nor was Bucky a young man. He was seventy-three, to be precise, and in very poor health. I had to wheel him into his workroom. I don't know why I'm telling you all this."

Lillian said, "Yes, let's talk about something cheerful." Glaring at Ralph.

Ralph raised his glass. "So welcome to Savage Point."

It was Angel Jones who pursued the subject. "It's always sudden, even if the one you love is going to die anyway. I remember I had an old horse once, his name was Sam, and he really didn't have many months to live, but I loved that old guy. Well, one night we had a fire in the barn—"

"An old *horse!*" Lillian exclaimed. "Are you comparing—?"

"You're right, it *is* sudden," Marlene said. "My father went suddenly when I was ten. I know the feeling."

Ralph said, "Who's ready for a refill?"

He stood up. No one else wanted a refill. He didn't really want one either, but he took his empty snifter back into the house. Teddy and Eileen were still sitting on the sofa, not looking at the football game. Ralph poured a half inch into his glass.

"What's the emblem on your jacket, Teddy?" he asked, peering at it. "The Virginia swimming team?"

"Oh, this," Teddy said, glancing down. "No, the family crest. My mother likes it. She had it put there." He covered it with his hand.

"Family is important in England," Eileen said.

"Both sides," Teddy said. He focused on the TV screen.

The Thatchers left a short time later, with measured smiles and gracious remarks. Teddy escorted his mother through the hedge.

"Hoity-toity," Lillian said.

Angel said, "Crème de la crème . . . curdled."

Ralph objected. "Oh, come on. That's just the way the English upper crust are. I sort of liked her."

"She's your type, Ralph," Lillian said.

Eileen said, "He's nice."

A few days later, Ralph asked Engelhart, "What made you run away from the English witch of the East?"

"Run away?" Fred said. "Is that what you think? That's incredible. I thought you knew me better than that. I don't run away. Didn't Angel tell you? I'm playing with plastic."

"Have it your way," Ralph said. "You missed hearing about her husband Bucky. Unlucky Bucky died in a fire."

"Where was she born?"

"If you heard her talk, you wouldn't ask that," Ralph said. "She's as English as her namesake Margaret."

"Did she say she was born there?"

"I don't remember. I'll ask her the next time I see her."

"It doesn't matter," Fred said.

"Maybe it does," Ralph said. "Your daughter seems to have been smitten by the Teddy boy."

"Yes, I know," Engelhart said.

* * *

Lillian paused at the corner of Center Drive and Dover Road to regroup. More fire engines were arriving and being directed up Dover. The din was dumbfounding. She started down Dover toward Savage Point Road, heading home. A fireman said, "You can't go down there, lady."

She said, "Go fight a fire, damn it!" and continued on her way.

Then the thought that had been scratching at her consciousness came out into the open. She wasn't thinking of Teddy Thatcher at all. She was thinking of her dumb, quixotic husband Ralph, who had jumped into the water and probably given himself a heart attack. And the thought came: *Teddy was an expert swimmer!* So why did he just stand there like a cigar store Indian when Eileen started swimming toward her father? He didn't want to get his nice jacket wet. No, he stood there frozen because his brain was immobilized like that of a woman before a closetful of clothes unable to decide what to put on. Strong-willed mother makes decisions for handsome son, son turns into zombie.

Ah, the hell with it.

Wait until I get my hands on that Ralph.

She pictured him dead, and she began sobbing.

5.

She arrived at an empty house. A scribbled note was taped to the front door: AT LIJ WITH EILEEN. SHE'S OK. BACK SOON. She sat down on the front step like a deflating blimp. She willed her mind to be blank, to ignore for the moment the inferno only a block away. She willed the tension out of her body. She drooped. Lillian Simmons sank into a sort of sleep, an exhausted stupor.

Fred Engelhart was in the sort of sleep called death. The volunteer ambulance corps had taken him and his daughter to Long Island Jewish Hospital. He was still in the ER, toe-tabbed DOA. When one of the residents insisted on examining Eileen instead of her father and talked of sending her to the burn unit at the Nassau County Medical Center, she punched him in the stomach. She was still in her damp swimsuit, shivering in the air-conditioning despite the shirt Ralph had put on her. "He's not *gone*! Bring him back! Do something! Don't keep saying he's *gone*!"

Ralph gently tugged her away from the doctor. "Take it easy, sweetie," he said. "They'll do what they can. You can't bring him back by slugging the doctor. Let's get something for those burns of yours."

"What burns?"

"Fat burns."

"What are you talking about?"

"A childhood joke. Here, sit in this wheelchair. Make out like you're sick."

"You're crazy, Uncle Ralph."

"Don't tell anybody."

A furtive movement drew Lillian's attention. There it was, crouched, tensed, under the hydrangea, an indistinct blur with glowering yellow eyes. Lillian straightened up. "Who are you?" she asked. The eyes glared, unblinking. The blur was grayish in color, but in the premature twilight under the moiling mountain of smoke all colors were dirty. "Are you Hunter?"

No response.

"Sorry, pussycat, I never can remember all your names." She stood up, and the cat crouched lower. "I don't blame you, Hunter, it's the end of the world. But it's also dinnertime. Didn't your mother—?"

She suddenly thought of the Cat Woman. "Oh, my God." She gazed through and over the trees on Dover Street to the flickering mass of smoke beyond, trying to picture exactly where the Cat Woman's house was. When Lillian had trudged around the fire in order to get home it had been bounded by Albemarle and Center Drive, but the path of the fire seemed to be widening as it advanced northeastward across the point.

"What's happening to your mother, Hunter? You live on Baycrest, right? She's probably safe up there, the fire won't reach that far north. Come on around back, feller, and I'll give you some tunafish. People tuna, not cat tuna. If you don't like it, that's tough."

She turned to go in the house. The cat remained where he was, peering balefully at a baleful world.

She took one more look at the sky. A helicopter flitted by overhead. Nothing else stirred except the hot southwest wind. She felt she was a spectator at a spectacle that was passing her by. Weird.

She went into the kitchen, turned on the small TV on top of the refrigerator, opened the can of tuna. An announcer was happily reciting the news. Murder in the Bronx. Then the man's voice quickened and rose, and the screen was filled with fire vehicles and smoke. The mayor in a red helmet, his face smudged, said something Lillian didn't get. The scene switched to an aerial shot of the great wind-whipped column of smoke with flickering licks of fire. The helicopter, of course.

The camera floated right over and almost into the smoke, fluttered in the turbulence, the lens zooming through breaks in the smoke to catch glimpses of people and firefighters on Center Drive. North of the fire the copter wheeled around over untouched suburban streets to make another run at the fire.

She found the pan that she reserved for feeding panhandling animals. She was on their list as a soft touch. She dumped the tuna into the pan. In the midst of destruction life goes on. Women's lot is to feed the survivors.

Kitty Henderson was preparing separate dinners for her thirteen children. She liked to think of them as her children. She had long since ceased bemoaning the stubborn finickiness of cats. They would rather die of starvation than eat something that wasn't congenial to their exquisitely sensitive palates. So she had separate bowls for each of the cats containing each one's favorite food. So much of her income from the old family trust went for cat food that there were months when she had to scrimp on her own food allowance.

A full half of her kitchen was devoted to the preparation of animal meals. As she shuffled from bowl to bowl, each Magic-Markered with a name, she hummed. "Onward Christian Soldiers" ... "Tea for Two" ... "When the Saints Come Marching In" ... "A Hundred Bottles of Beer on the Wall" ... "Amazing Grace" ... "A Pretty Girl Is Like a Melody" ... "Row, Row, Row Your Boat" ... "Yankee Doodle Dandy" ... "Yes, Sir, She's My Baby" ... and "Boom-Da-Da-Boom" (Beethoven's Fifth). And so the medley went, the tunes subconsciously suggested by the cats' names and personalities—Blackie, Freshie, Long John, Evel Knevel,

Hunter, Tiger, Mama, Mathilda, Ugly, Bobtail, Homer, Bo Peep, and Snooty. Three of them, Evel Knevel, Hunter, and Tiger, were wild because Mama neglected to bring that litter around for the necessary people orientation until they were too old.

Kitty Henderson moved slowly. She was in her late eighties, with swollen ankles and arthritic joints, one good eye, the other walled off by a cataract, a tiny woman with bony arms, a bloated body. She was one of the regular stop-offs for Ralph Simmons on his daily walks. "I take in strays," she told Ralph with a laugh; "that's all you can say." She was not given to self-analysis.

But Ralph summed her up for Lillian. "Unaccustomed as I am to jiffy diagnoses—"

"Hah!"

"—and despite snorts of derision from the uninformed masses, our beloved Cat Woman is acting from a frustrated maternal instinct—"

"What do you know about maternal instincts, old man?"

"—a lonely person's need for companionship, and the satisfaction of doing something well. She's good at what she does. Now, regarding sex—"

"What sex? She's eighty-eight, for crying out loud."

"—and still a virgin. Wait, let me go on. She was married about seventy years ago, she told me that, but it was quickly annulled. Maybe he got in, maybe he didn't. What I think is, she's timidly curious about us male creatures and covers it by clicking and winking as if she were the Wife of Bath."

"I think *you* ought to take a bath, Ralph."

What Ralph didn't know was that Kitty Henderson's latest stray was her next-door neighbor, Todd Gilchrist. He reminded her of Ugly, her favorite cat, a battered old tomcat with a crumpled ear and a perpetually oozing eye. The difference was that Ugly had lived a full life, whereas she suspected that Gilchrist's was wasted. Which made Gilchrist all the more in need of her caring. He came to her in the dark of night so none of the neighbors would see, and he would spill out the brimming bile that was in him and then relate, "hark back to," the high times he had had with Ellie, his dear wife who had fallen down the cellar stairs.

Kitty didn't mind seeing his house going to wrack and ruin next door. She scarcely noticed the deterioration, since her own house was quite shabby. Smelly too. She wished she could help Todd Gilchrist with his money problems. There's no money in cats, she said. Don't worry, she told him; your ship will come in.

She worried about him. She hadn't seen him for a week now. She wished he wouldn't drink so much. She must speak to him about that. God must be a little out of sorts with him, and she feared for him in the afterlife. She must help him find amazing grace. Yes. She must devote her life to saving his.

The cats were acting strangely. Kitty Henderson generally fed them in the backyard or, in case of rain, on the back porch. But today they all wanted to come in the house. Those that were in the vicinity, that is. Some of them had disappeared—Long John and Mathilda in addition to the three wild ones. Blackie, Freshie, and the rest congregated on the back porch, but when Kitty put down their bowls, they weren't interested in eating.

"All right, come on in, you miserable beasties," she said, and she laboriously lugged the bowls back into the kitchen. Some ate, some didn't. They moved about restlessly, then froze in a listening position, then padded through the house and, one by one, disappeared. The Cat Woman was disturbed.

"You're not eating, Ugly," she said to the beat-up tom. "Don't you feel good? What's the matter with the others? They're all acting crazy." In her experience the only time the cats had acted like this was during the hurricane, and that was twenty or thirty years ago.

"Nobody said anything about a hurricane," she muttered.

She went out into the backyard and looked up. No, just the same darn hot wind that they'd had for months, it seemed like. She looked south and saw the big cloud there.

"Well, I'll be. That must be it. Sounds like thunder too. My, my," she said and shook her head. Her one good eye was tearing.

She went back into the house without looking at the Gilchrist house next door.

Judith the architect stood on the corner of Center Drive and Dover Street and watched without visible emotion the destruction of her house by fire a block away. Her husband sat on the curb. He was weeping softly. She reached down absently and patted his head. "There, there," she said, not looking at him.

"Everything we own, Jude," he said.

"I know. It's not so bad."

"My book," he said.

"You have it right there," she said.

He was hugging a thick manila folder on his lap. "But my research," he said.

She patted his head harder than she intended. "Out of the ashes," she said in the voice of a visionary. "We'll build a whole new life, dear, out of the ashes. Few people get the chance to cut away all the accumulated junk of the past. Right there—"

She pointed at the blazing house.

"Right there we'll build the house that would turn Frank Lloyd Wright green with envy. Not like the monstrosity that Engelhart built. No, a house that people will come from all over to look at . . ."

"I liked the old house," he said.

She didn't hear him. She was looking at a house being built. It was going to be magnificent.

Rudolf Mannheim's house stood on a rise at a point where the shoreline curved to the northeast. It was out of reach of the fire. Besides, it was a stone house with a slate roof, almost impregnable to fire from the outside. From its second-floor deck, Mannheim had a panoramic view of the bay down to its mouth to the south.

A hazy sun was low on the opposite shore, and he had to use his hand as a visor to watch the progress of the red fireboat as it approached the Savage Point dock. He had heard the expression, "a spit in the ocean," and he thought that was what the contribution of the boat's stream of water would be to controlling the fire—a spit in the ocean. He had an unobstructed view of the turbulence where Engelhart's house had been; as for the rest of it, he could only see the great bank of smoke rolling east over the intervening forest of trees. Well, at least the fireboat would keep the fire from veering north and threatening his own house and those of his neighbors. Some of those neighbors were congregated on Shore Road below him, peering south in consternation.

Mannheim stood erect on the deck above them, feeling tall, a commanding presence. He was a psychologist who had little insight, or refused to acknowledge what insights he had, into his own mental mechanisms. He was a short man, five seven, who somehow saw himself as Moses coming down from the mountain holding the stone tablets. It was a necessary image to him if he were to function in his profession. He liked the feel of the wind tousling his beard, which he had grown decades ago because he believed that his chin was a damnably weak one that didn't fit the image.

He had little in common with Fred Engelhart. The uneasiness had always been there from the time they had been comrades in arms in an ignoble cause. Fred was all impulse, while Rudolf was all caution. Today he was uncomfortable about the way he had conducted himself in the boat. He had lost his command presence.

He took his pipe from his pocket, filled it with tobacco that smelled like molasses, tamped it down. As he held the flaming match over the bowl, the match pad was in the other hand. FINE FOOD PRODUCTS—WHITE ROSE, said the match pad. He thought of Eric Bushman, then tried to push him out of his mind. Unlike Ralph Simmons who walked, the much older Bushman kept in shape by jogging relentlessly, in heat and cold, rain and snow; the bullet-headed man went by Mannheim's house twice a day. Yet the retired foreign service officer was popular in Savage Point society for the amusing tales he told of the many countries he had served in.

The fireboat started shooting its awesome stream of water high in the air. For all its power, however, the stream could not quite reach the fire at Engelhart's. It swung inland.

Mannheim went downstairs where he put on his rain slicker and hat. Prudence was sitting in her rocking chair gazing into the dead fireplace, some neglected knitting in her lap. She had witnessed as much of the turmoil as she thought necessary and had come in the house to meditate. Her husband told her he was going down the road to get a better look at what was going on.

"You're going to Bushman's, aren't you?" she said.

"I might see him." He was studying himself in the hall mirror. He looked like the captain of an old New England fishing boat.

"It might be wise to stay away from him, Rudolf," she said quietly.

"I said I might see him, I didn't say I would. I just want to see how bad the fire is."

She said, "Be careful."

"You know me," he said.

He went out the front door, down the steps to the road. Acknowledging the murmured comments of neighbors, he marched down Shore Road, past the dock, through the mist beneath the overarching stream of water from the fireboat, to the bend in the road where it turned away from the shore to end at Savage Point Road.

Eric Bushman's house was thoroughly wetted down with water from the fireboat. The gangling man stood in his front doorway, peering around in outrage.

"Bushman!"

The slickered figure of Rudolf Mannheim stood below him in the road.

"Is that you, Mannheim?"

Mannheim pushed the hat away from his face. He disliked being on the low ground, but he was not going to step onto Bushman's property.

"The bloody Gauleiter died over forty years ago," Mannheim said in a loud voice. "His order has no force here."

Bushman shook his head, an expression of contempt on his face. "Still singing the same old song," he said. "I told you—"

"Was it you?" Mannheim shouted.

Bushman waved him away in disgust.

"Did you kill Engelhart?"

Bushman said, "Just listen to yourself, little man. The psychologist is crazy in the head. Here comes the water again. This wonderful city is saving us from the fire by polluting us with the bay water. Look up and open your mouth. I advise that you do that."

Bushman backed into the house and closed the door.

Mannheim stood alone in the dripping mist. Undecided. Still cautious.

6.

Inexorably the swath of the fire widened as it raged across the middle of Savage Point. It took only the two houses on the north side of Schmidt's Lane—Engelhart's and his hostile neighbor's—and the unoccupied brick house on the corner of Savage Point Road, killing the neighbor and his aged wife in addition to Fred and Angel. After leaping the road it engaged hedges, bushes, trees, and twelve more houses, including that of Judith the architect. The firemen tried to save the houses on the far side of Center Drive, but it was spit in the ocean, and they were driven back.

Captain Tom Noonan's Engine Company 114, stationed on Dover road, punched at the southern flank of the fire with their inch-and-a-half line to slow the mighty conflagration's expansion toward the south. Other engine companies were fighting the same battle farther east.

Noonan viewed the mayor as a humorous hambone but gave him credit for appointing a career firefighter as commissioner. He had given credibility to his administration by appointing the much decorated Zimmer, downplaying the fact that the two had grown up together in the same area of Chelsea and were poker-playing buddies. So it was Commissioner Zimmer who took charge of operations at the Great Savage Point Fire.

Dover Street, the main street across the base of Savage Point, was clogged with apparatus, so Zimmer had to route backup companies up narrow side streets to circumnavigate the fire, some to fight it head-on from East Drive, others to proceed farther north to attack the fire's northern perimeter. He also mobilized his meager helicopter fleet to bomb the fire with water from above. This was about as effective as drunken conventioneers dropping paper bags of water from hotel windows. The firefighters fought bravely, the rescue squads saved some lives, but the water main to the point was never designed to accommodate such a demand for water, and the pressure diminished almost to the vanishing point.

The southwest wind whistled, and the fire monster charged on, its roar reaching the impacted density of a train speeding through a tunnel.

When Lillian Simmons took the dish of people tuna to the backyard, Hunter the cat failed to appear. As she peered around in the gloom, however, she saw that the whole yard was alive with other creatures. On the ground and in the trees, squirrels moved sluggishly, then froze for long minutes; a mother raccoon plodded across the lawn followed by three small ones; two rabbits cowered in the foliage ("Hey, I thought you were all gone," she said to them); birds chittered and fluttered in the trees; a single male pheasant lumbered away only to circle around and come back; a sickly pale mound turned out to be an opossum playing possum; a rat scurried through the hedge to the Thatcher property. Hunter finally showed up with a friend.

"Holy mackerel," she said, "we're a camp for displaced animals."

She went back into the house, thinking, *What do squirrels eat? Nuts. Raccoons? Garbage. Rabbits? Lettuce, or is it carrots? The opossum is on his own. The rats can go screw themselves.* She brought back what food she could find and scattered it in the yard.

"Eat," she commanded. "Or I'll kill you."

She noticed Marlene Thatcher coming around the side of her house from the front.

"Isn't this terrible?" Lillian called to her.

The woman stopped. "Yes. Of course. Brutal."

Lillian moved to the hedge, scattering some squirrels. Marlene Thatcher remained where she was. Lillian said, "I see you've been invaded too. I was just feeding some of them. They seem so—stunned."

"During the war we had only rats," the woman said. "The bombs made the rats go mad." She made a disgusted sound.

"Where was that?" Lillian asked.

The woman said, "What? Oh, in London, of course. As a little girl, I thought it was the rat capital of the world." She moved toward her back entrance. "I must be getting in."

Lillian called, "Where's Teddy?"

Marlene Thatcher paused. "He followed the girl to the hospital."

It was only after the woman had disappeared into the house that Lillian realized that what Marlene Thatcher had in her hand was a wine glass.

Ralph Simmons was glad when Ted Thatcher arrived at the hospital. He had helped guide Eileen through the interminable formalities of death in a civilized country. He had been through it before with Margaret, and it had seemed to him that the goal of most of the red tape was to nail down who was going to pay for what. Eileen's burns proved to be no worse than a mild sunburn with scattered spots of deeper burns. She had calmed down when her intelligence finally accepted the reality that her father was dead and that nothing could be done to bring him back.

Teddy was in the waiting room when they came out of Emergency. Eileen looked at him and looked away. For the last half hour she had spoken only in grunts and monosyllables. Her eyes were teary and red-rimmed, but she hadn't wept. Her jaw was clamped shut.

Teddy had changed into slacks and a short-sleeved

shirt. He stood stiffly, a pleading look on his face. "I'm sorry, love," he mumbled. "I acted rottenly."

"No sweat," she said. She turned to Ralph. "Are we through here, Uncle Ralph?"

Ralph nodded and guided her through the sliding door out into the twilight. Teddy followed. He put a hand on Ralph's arm.

"What can I do to help?" he pleaded. "I've got to do something. Tell me. I feel so—helpless." The last word quivered as it come out.

"There's not much to do, Ted," Ralph said. "Eileen is coming home with us."

"Let me drive her. Please, Eileen, let me drive you. If you don't, I'll feel like a stinker." Wisely he didn't touch her.

Eileen shrugged. She went with him to his Trans-Am. Ralph looked around the parking lot for his own Skyhawk, suddenly remembered that he had come in the ambulance and that his car was still at the Savage Point dock. He had wanted to leave the two young people alone to make their peace, but he wanted even more strongly not to be stranded miles from home.

He ran after Ted and Eileen and crowded into the car with them. Eileen sat in the middle. Nobody spoke while they rode up Lakeville Road and swung onto the expressway for the short stretch to Savage Point Road. North of Northern Boulevard there was a police roadblock at the railroad overpass.

At Ralph's suggestion Ted parked the car near the train station, and they walked from there past the school and church, through clusters of onlookers and officials and around emergency vehicles parked off the roadway. Several acquaintances asked, "Did it get your house, Ralph?" and he told them, "No, thank God."

The corner of Dover and Savage Point Road was so jammed with people and vehicles that they bypassed the intersection by going down the lane at the rear of their properties and entering through the backyards.

Lillian met them at the back porch, peered anxiously

at each of them in the gathering dusk. "Everything all right?" she asked.

Ralph said, "Jim-dandy."

Ted stood before Eileen. "Take care," he said, and she said, "Yes." Ralph figured that the rift was being healed slowly. Ted went through the hedge to his own home, and Lillian shooed Ralph and Eileen into the house, where she offered Eileen some chicken soup. Eileen took a cold Coke instead and held it to her forehead. Ralph settled for a belt of bourbon, which he downed quickly.

Nobody felt like eating. Lillian put Eileen under a warm shower, then ten minutes later had to take her out and dry her. She found a pair of jeans and a blouse that had belonged to her daughter and helped Eileen put them on. Then she took them off again and put the passive girl to bed in one of the spare rooms.

"She worries me," she said to Ralph.

Ralph was sprawled on the sofa, holding a second bourbon. "She'll be all right," he said. "It's a sort of healing process . . . I hope."

They were in the living room with the windows and doors closed and the air-conditioning on. The sounds of the fire and the firefighting were remote. Ralph tried to think of something else and couldn't. "Where's the car?" he asked.

"Still at the dock," she told him.

"I suppose I ought to go get it."

"For pity sake, Ralph, you know you can't get through."

He sighed. "I loved having drinks in the bell tower."

"So did I."

"I miss him already."

"How about a chicken sandwich? You have to eat something."

He ate half a sandwich, then said, "I'm going to see if the car is all right." He stood up.

"You're a nut."

He went out the door. "I won't be long," he said.

Weird. Night had fallen on Dover Street, and he

could see stars in the hazy sky. But only a few hundred feet to the north a great, churning, clamorous cloud covered heaven and earth, its interior illuminated with the reds and yellows of uncontrolled fires.

He felt an all-consuming sense of awe, and his mind moved to thoughts of apocalypse. Maybe it's the beginning of the end. Maybe God got fed up with us again and decided to cleanse the earth by fire, starting with the middle-class sinners of Savage Point.

Ralph wasn't the only one with thoughts of apocalypse. Penelope Potter saw fire and brimstone, not in a vision but in actuality, raging two hundred feet away on East Drive, clutching at her house with fiery fingers, bombarding it with flaming missiles, while crouched firefighters sprayed it—and nearby buildings—with uncertain streams of water.

She and her husband, Philemon, sat in camp chairs provided by that nice Jewish family. There was a time not too long ago when Jewish people, no matter how nice, were blackballed at the club. But all that was gone now. So they sat like lumpen royalty on the nice front lawn in ringside thrones, viewing the greatest fire in New York City's history. She glanced at her husband; his stony features seemed to move in the rippling red glow of the fire. For a fleeting instant he was the statue of St. Joseph in the Dresden Cathedral during the firestorm of Allied bombardment . . .

She was confident that her brick house would repel the onslaught and survive. She saw it in her mind standing there in the aftermath, magnificently intact, saved by God, while all around was devastation. She took little satisfaction in this but rather was filled with dismay because she was greatly afraid that two of her favorite people were lost.

Don and Betsy Grant were the magically beautiful couple who lived across the street in the exquisitely lovely little house made of gingerbread. To her they were people out of the fairy tales of her childhood, not Hansel and Gretel or any other specific twosome but the generic prince and princess who lived happily ever after.

Firemen told her that people were trapped in the Grant house. Don and Betsy had had no children, sadly, so the trapped people could only be them. Penelope had truly believed that Don and Betsy would live happily ever after, and she was shaken by this nasty twist of fate. It was almost as if one of her predictions had turned catastrophically wrong.

She prayed desperately for a miracle, but even as she prayed she knew that the prince and princess were lost—ignominiously.

"Are you all right, Penny?"

A man came up from the sidewalk and sat heavily on the lawn beside her. The only man who ever called her Penny was Ralph Simmons.

She said, "The world of make-believe is vanishing before our eyes, Mr. Simmons. It's time has come, I'm afraid."

She recalled Ralph Simmons once saying to her that the God-fearing people of Savage Point were living in a world of make-believe: they worked hard in the outside world and tried to instill the same work ethic in their children, but the parents' very success, measured by money and creature comforts, doomed many of the kids to be comfortable failures.

Ralph peered down East Drive. "That's Don and Betsy's house," he said.

Penelope Potter said, "Two firemen went in and never came out, God rest their souls."

Ralph shook his head wearily. Don and Betsy were beautiful but useless; the firemen may not have been pretty but they were useful. It wasn't a fair trade-off.

Don and Betsy were in their upstairs bedroom. Fifteen minutes earlier two firemen with axes had broken in downstairs and told Don to get the hell out. Don had said that his wife was upstairs, he would go up and get her, and he had quickly run up the stairs. The firemen hesitated, then belatedly decided that it was their job to see that the wife got out. They started to clump up the stairs when the flashover occurred and the whole staircase was in flames. They made it to the foot of the stairs, where they died of scorched lungs.

Don made it to the bedroom at the back of the house, saw the fire charge up the stairs after him, and he slammed the bedroom door to cut it off. Betsy lay on the bed propped against the headboard, curled on her side, the only position she found comfortable. Her breathing was labored.

"Hey, Sleeping Beauty," Don said.

The heat in the room was building, and smoke was seeping in, under the door on one side and spiraling from the baseboard under the windows in the back. The kitchen extension beneath the windows had been intact the last time he had looked, but now the view was of smoke and flame.

"I'm not asleep," Betsy said, without stirring from her curled position.

Don looked at her and thought how truly lovely she was, even now. She had lost a lot of weight in recent months, and women at the club had asked what diet she was on. She could have replied, "Cancer," but she didn't. To Don, the skin over the delicate bones of her face was incredibly beautiful.

She said, "Your hair is mussed."

He slicked his hair with his hand.

She said, "I like it that way," and she smiled.

He said, "We're supposed to get out of here, and we can't."

Don Grant was not very bright, but he knew that, barring a miracle, they were going to die. He was a successful male model, and his whole life, from childhood, had consisted of surfaces. He had a brain that was unused, and his emotions were skin-deep. He loved Betsy for her beauty.

He went to sit on the bed beside her, and she mumbled, "Careful, Donny." Then she said, "I wet the bed."

He laughed. "Should have saved it for the fire."

She coughed dryly, shallowly.

He got the water glass from the side table, held the gooseneck straw to her lips, and she drank.

The wall-to-wall carpeting seemed to be shimmering, and he pulled his feet onto the bed. He laughed, saying, "It's not only you, Bets. Looks like I'm going with you."

She said, "Together. That's nice." Then she said, "You don't mind?"

"Of course not. I couldn't live without you."

"I wanted you to find a nice girl."

"I wouldn't dream," he said.

He curled on the bed beside her. He felt her heart beating rapidly, hastening blood to her useless lungs for oxygen that wasn't there. They had known for six months that she had a rare form of lung cancer, congenital in nature, that had nothing to do with smoking. Betsy, the perfect princess, did not smoke. They had told no one at the club. It was their secret.

Now the smoke was sending her into paroxysms of coughing and gasping. The room was opaque. Don tried breathing through the sheet to mask out the smoke. It didn't work. His own lungs were becoming as diseased as hers. He noticed that she was in extreme distress.

He raised himself on an elbow, clutched a pillow. "Bets," he gasped. "Let me . . . stop it." He held the pillow over her head.

She weakly pushed it away. " 'S' wrong," she said. "Jus' hold me."

He held her.

The door burst into flame.

We should pray, she thought. *Now I lay me . . . no, us . . . lay us down to sleep . . .* He was losing consciousness. He felt Betsy stop breathing. *Thank you for marrying me*—then he was unconscious.

Don and Betsy died peacefully and lived happily ever after. No one would ever know because it was their secret.

Ralph Simmons got to his feet. He squeezed Penelope Potter's frail shoulder. "Take care, my child," he said to the old woman. It amused him to reverse roles in his speech.

Without looking at the other figures standing there in the darkness glazed with shock, he walked wearily on. He knew that the goal of his lonely ramble, his odyssey around the fire, was dumb—to get to Shore Road to see his car. There was no way he could drive it home and no sense in going to look at it. Yet it was impossible for him to stay home and do nothing.

7.

Penelope Potter was the other outsider who claimed she had seen the white rose. Ralph's daily stroll frequently took him past her house, and about once a week she would invite him in for a chat, saying that his lighthearted gab relieved her heavy pondering and cheered her up. Ralph was sure, however, that the real reason was to find out what was going on in Savage Point, since she had scant contact with her neighbors. For his part, he delighted in following the darting zigzags of her thought processes and the unexpected nonsequiturs. He didn't know whether she was a sincere fraud or an out-and-out charlatan.

Now as he plodded through the dark and eerie landscape toward his stranded car, he recalled his latest visit with the woman. Could it have been only three or four days ago?

This time she was openly curious about a specific neighbor, Todd Gilchrist. She said that Gilchrist, a man she scarcely knew, had come to her uninvited a week earlier, in such a disturbed state of mind that he had frightened her. There was a knot of concentration above her eyes as she told of the visit, relating every detail as if she were cross-examining herself and didn't know which detail was significant and which wasn't.

Ralph found himself being lulled—dulled—until Fred Engelhart's name was mentioned.

Penelope had said she wanted to get Ralph's reaction, but as the story droned on, he realized she was telling it to clarify her own reaction, not to get his.

Penelope Potter was a holy woman. The *National Enquirer* said so several times a year when it published her predictions with much promotional hoopla. She was initially canonized in 1968 when she predicted the assassination of Martin Luther King. She called it a revelation, as distinguished from precognition. She had been alone in a darkened church, feeling strangely disquieted, when she saw a vision. As it became clearer in the motes of a sunbeam, she saw that it was a man nailed to a cross—a black man! The man's chest burst open, and he expired. The experience was a transcendental high, and she hastened home to write it down. Being experienced in the prediction business and knowing the need for a safety cop-out, she did not identify the man by name but wrote that it was "a leading Negro personality" who was crucified. A week after publication the Reverend King was martyred in Memphis, and millions of people across the country concluded that Penelope Potter had foreseen the bloody event. And over the years Penelope came to believe that she truly had, erasing from her mind the face that she had actually seen—that of the actor Sidney Poitier, as she had seen him in *Guess Who's Coming to Dinner*.

Faithfully every morning she had her secretary drive her to the Savage Point Episcopal Church, where she sat humbly in a rear pew, a tiny figure with dyed brown hair, round peasant face, and pale blue eyes, and she prayed to God for a renewal of her powers of prognostication. Unfortunately the ways of the Lord are inscrutable, and she was never sure whether He was answering her or not. In the ensuing year, therefore, she couched her more daring predictions in the tongue of Nostradamus so that they could apply to a variety of individuals and situations and be interpreted accordingly; the rest were fish-in-a-barrel gossip—Liz Taylor and Zsa Zsa Gabor would marry again, Los Angeles would have an earthquake that would threaten to slide it into the sea, a singing star would O.D. on drugs, a sexual scandal would smear a prominent politician, and communist sympathizers were infiltrating (a) the New York Philharmonic, (b) the Pentagon, (c) the Kremlin, and (d) the National Education Association. Just as the public was losing interest in the Potter predictions she came up with "a leading Hollywood personality will die of AIDS," and she was once more the public's favorite seer. And, too, Penelope Potter once more believed in her powers.

Her home was a large, gloomy Tudor on the high ground of Savage Point. The week before the Engelhart house explosion, her secretary and companion Henrietta, a pale thing with pale red hair, stopped the pale gray BMW in the driveway, and Penelope Potter hopped out like a spry child, belying her years. There was much speculation about her age. Her authorized biographical sheet put her age at sixty-three, but there were many who claimed she was ten, even twenty years older than that. Whatever her age, she moved quickly. Like Peter Rabbit, she scampered.

In the main hall she peered into her husband's office, as she always did. Philemon Potter sat erect at his mahogany desk, unmoving, his bowl of cornflakes before him, untouched. He had a strong face with a great masculine nose, his gray hair neatly combed in waves. Garbed in dark, ultraconservative clothing, he could have been a diplomat or an undertaker. In actuality, he was the leading real-estate broker in Savage Point, with most of his clients drawn to him by the reputation of his mystical wife. She gazed at his profile and believed him to be the handsomest man in creation. She once had a religious card depicting St. Joseph, and the picture was the spitting image of her dear husband. She thought of him as St. Joseph.

"Eat your breakfast, darling," she said.

He moved a finger.

She sighed and moved on to her own atelier, a cavernous, high-ceilinged room with a large stained-glass window at one end and dark furnishings throughout. The window was an impressionistic view of a woman in a pale blue gown levitating, rising from earth below to heaven above, presumably representing the Assumption of Mary, though the woman's face bore a vague resemblance to Penelope herself.

She took off her white gloves, sat at her desk, and turned on the lamp. Her day's correspondence had been placed on the desk by Henrietta in two neat stacks, one sacred, the other profane. She put on her rimless glasses and, with a thrill of anticipation, dug in. One never knew where one's next inspiration would come from. Henrietta brought in Penelope's customary cup of tea and silently sat in her chair beside the desk.

The gushing fan letters she disposed of quickly with a few words to Henrietta indicating which form reply to use. The more interesting communications came from police departments as well as individuals asking for help in locating missing loved ones. These letters frequently enclosed an article of clothing or some other possession of the missing person. She had had some success in the past by reporting the vibrations she received and the images that formed in her mind. She cautiously refrained from interpreting the phenomena ever since the embarrassing time when she assured a woman in Little Rock that her daughter was alive and well in New Orleans only to have the police find the poor girl's rotted corpse in a wooded area a mile from home.

She had just finished her dictation when the doorbell chimed.

A minute later Henrietta escorted the visitor to the atelier. Penelope studied him in the dim light, received a tingle of disaster, put her hand to her forehead, and said, "Don't tell me—Bill Mahoney." She held out her hand.

The man hesitantly took her hand. "Todd Gilchrist,

Miss Potter," he said in a muted barroom voice. "Bill Mahoney moved to Florida last spring."

Oh, dear.

"Yes, yes," she said. "I remember. Why don't we sit over here?" She took his arm and propelled him to where a sofa, chair, and coffee table formed a conversation area.

This once-handsome man is an alcoholic, she said to herself, noting the bloodshot eyes, the pouches under them, and the slack posture of the shoulders. He was dressed in a brown business suit with shirt and tie, slightly rumpled; his sparse hair was slightly rumpled too. She sat in the chair, he sat on the edge of the sofa.

He squared his shoulders, and she caught a sense of smoldering anger. A touchy situation.

"I met you last spring at the strawberry festival up at the church," he said. "But I'm sure you meet so many people that—"

"Tut, tut," she said. "I remember you very well. Yes, indeed."

"Bill Mahoney had a heart attack, and he had to retire," he went on. "People often said that we looked alike, but he was a lot older than me. I'm only fifty, and I guess I'm beginning to look my age." He smiled painfully.

"Yes." She studied him in silence.

He shifted his position, cleared his throat.

"I was hoping—" he said. "First, let me apologize for bothering you. I'm a great fan of yours, and I'm in what you might call an emergency situation, sort of a midlife crisis—" He laughed nervously.

Oh, dear. Sex.

"What I mean is—is there any way you can predict my future? I'm really up in the air, er, in a blind alley, no, you can't be up in the air and in a blind alley, can you? . . . Look, you predict things, it's a great gift, precognition you call it—I'd be very grateful if you would, what?—just look at me or touch my hand or whatever you do, and tell me something, anything about, well, *me*, show me the way out. I know you don't take customers, but, being a neighbor and all, I was hoping—"

He stopped speaking and gazed at her with liquid eyes, both pleading and demanding.

She said, "I don't want to give you false hope, Mr. Gilchrist—my powers are greatly exaggerated. But tell me about yourself, and we'll see."

He looked lost. "Where should I begin?"

"Anywhere . . . Are you married?"

"She died."

"Oh, dear. Any children?"

"He died."

Seeing that he was about to burst into tears, she said quickly, "I can understand how that might, as they say, knock you for a loop, losing your wife and son, but I think the person who can be most helpful to you is Father Babson—"

He held up his hand, shaking his head. "I can't even communicate properly anymore. And that's my field, communications. Or that *was* my field." He took a deep breath, let it out.

"My wife died ten years ago, my son six months ago, and I'm not an Episcopalian even though I went to your strawberry festival. I don't even like strawberries. I went with a lady friend. I called her my strawberry blonde. And now she's left me. I ran out of money, and she left me. You want to find out who your real friends are? Run out of money! Do you want to know how many friends I have on Savage Point? Zero! Zilch! Nada!"

She sneaked a look at her watch.

He said, "Ah-*hah*!"

She stiffened. "I am not about to kick you out of here," she said with dignity. "But I do have things to do. I would be happy if you would get to the point . . . Is it money?"

"That's part of it, Miss Potter," Gilchrist said, easing back an inch on the sofa. "My whole world has blown up in my face, sort of a slow-motion explosion over the course of ten years, but an explosion just the same.

Let's say it started with the death of my wife. That's as good a place as any. Ellie and I had some good times together. I was bringing home good money . . .

"I was the P.R. man, the public-relations man in the city for a big company, a Fortune 500 company, a mountain of a company climbing into the mist. I was the glad-hander. My job was to go to the bars where the newspaper guys hang out, places like Charley O's and Costello's, and make friends with these guys and buy them drinks and tell them jokes—I was pretty good at telling jokes—and make them think my company was a prince among companies. I was its goodwill ambassador, that's what I was, and it's not something you can point to specifically, but I know there were many times my work resulted in a good press when the company needed it badly, the crooked bastards! Did I say Fortune 500? It was Misfortune 500 for me!

"Anyway, Ellie couldn't hold her liquor. We had a lot of great parties, and she was the life of the party, and one night she fell down the cellar stairs and cracked her head open. Why she wanted to go down to the cellar I don't remember, but anyway my dear, fun-loving wife passed away. You know, I loved her, I really did. She was my pal, my buddy, if you know what I mean."

For a moment his gaze was on something, memories, over Penelope's head. He pulled it back down.

"So I had to be both father and mother to Brian, he was something like eight at the time. The whole thing is a haze, and I don't want to take up too much of your time. But the kid was bound to be affected, and I guess I wasn't there when he needed me. Anyway, I guess he must have been fifteen when I found out he was on drugs. He was a bright kid, but he got in with the wrong crowd. Boys. He had no girlfriends, I guess that was part of it. These kids were on beer and drugs. Poison.

"Well, I clamped down on Brian. I spent more time with him. I showed him that drugs were suicide, and I tried to show him how to know his capacity when it came to booze. It took a long time, and I thought he was coming out of it when the accident happened . . .

"I'll throw two names at you. Bruce Webster."

Penelope nodded. "I know the Websters."

"Fred Engelhart."

"Yes, the strange one."

"Well, this Bruce son of a bitch, if you'll pardon the expression, was four years older than my Brian, and he had Brian under his thumb. He's the one who brought crack around and got Brian on it. It's possible I might kill that snotty bastard some day—"

"Mr. Gilchrist!" Penelope exclaimed, frightened by the look on the man's face.

He refocused on her. "Sorry, Miss Potter—I'm a forgiving man, but not when it comes to that person. I never had ulcers until this happened. But I blame this crazy Engelhart guy almost as much, this wild man from Borneo. He doesn't belong here. He's a disruptive element. Kids can be cruel sometimes, they like to pick on outsiders. They played jokes on Engelhart, dead cat on his doorstep, things like that. I don't blame them."

"So this night they were in Bruce's car, and they decided to scare this fellow Engelhart. They backed the car into Schmidt's Lane so they were facing out, and they threw the most powerful firecrackers they had at Engelhart's house. Well, he came running out, and this Webster nitwit gunned his car, and Engelhart came running after them like a monster from one of those movies. I'm convinced that if he hadn't chased them, it wouldn't have happened.

"The car came screeching out of the lane onto Savage Point Road and rammed into a telephone pole on the other side. Bruce didn't have a scratch. My Brian had his head split open. Just like his mother." He stopped talking.

Penelope stirred. "How tragic. But I still don't see how I—" Her voice trailed off.

He was glaring at her. "The day before the accident my big-hearted company gave me the can. After twenty years of busting my tail for them, they did it by interoffice memo. Twenty years! Do you know what my boss said? He said, 'That's the way the cookie crumbles.' He thought he was being sympathetic. The only human being there was his secretary. She gave me a flower."

"A white rose," Penelope said.

He frowned. "No. It was a yellow thing. I don't know flowers from a hole in the ground. Ellie was the one who knew flowers. The thing is, when the cops told me about Brian I was three sheets to the wind. Everything was piling up at once. I know how to hold my liquor, but that night I'd let go, you can understand that. They tell me I tried to sock the cop, that's how far gone I was."

"Are you sure it wasn't a white rose?" She had seen the flower so clearly.

Gilchrist went on with his recital, not hearing the question.

"The funeral cost me seven thousand dollars. Last month I missed a payment on the mortgage. Maybe the month before too. Yesterday I got a nasty letter from the bank. After eighteen years without missing a payment I get a nasty letter, can you imagine that? I called and told the pipsqueak who answered that I was a little strapped and couldn't we refinance the thing. It only has seven more years to run. He said they had looked at the house and it was in such a state of disrepair they couldn't see sending good money after bad. So I lost my temper and said some things I shouldn't. They're going to foreclose."

Penelope Potter looked at him with mixed pity and repulsion. The man smelled of alcohol and decomposition. But a stronger sense was taking hold of her, her business sense. After all, she and her dear husband were in the real-estate business.

She said, "I'm terribly, terribly sorry for you, Mr. Gilchrist. I'll pray for you . . . I take it from what you said that your only asset is your house."

He sighed. "That's about the size of it. Nobody wants

to hire a middle-aged P.R. man. It's a young man's game. Maybe I should become a shoe salesman."

"Try not to be bitter," she said. "Look on the bright side. You can always sell your house."

He stiffened. "No. That would be telling the whole town I'm a loser. I don't have much left, but I have this pig-headed pride. I have the place insured for three hundred thousand, but that bank is after my blood, and I have a few other debts, and I wouldn't get a fraction of that. What good would that do?"

From sympathetic listener she had been now shifted to brisk businesswoman. "Come now, you'd get even less if you let them foreclose. You came for my advice, Mr. Gilchrist, and I say spruce it up a little, slap a coat of paint on it as my husband says, and put it up for sale."

He was shaking his head. "Not three hundred thou."

"You'd be surprised. Real-estate prices have gone through the roof. Some bare lots are going for over three hundred thousand. Bare lots! So if your house is basically sound . . ."

"It might come to that, Miss Potter, but—"

"You don't have much time. The bank—"

"I know, I know," he said. "It's possible I may come back tomorrow and say, 'Sell my house.' But right now I can't think clearly. I took a short snort for breakfast. That generally clears my head. But it didn't. I still feel strung out. Here, touch my hand, go in a trance or whatever you do, and tell me."

He was leaning toward her, hand outstretched. His agonized face was only inches from hers. Reluctantly she touched the back of his hand.

She said, "You have anger in your heart. I see that you want to strike back. At your company, your former boss, the Webster boy. Mr. Engelhart. In fact, everybody in Savage Point who has deserted you. I think you misread your neighbors, but that doesn't change the way you feel, does it?"

She spoke quickly, almost without thinking, saying anything to soothe the bedeviled man and get him out of her house before he turned violent. He was obviously a fallen Catholic who had come to her as he would in earlier years have gone to a priest in confession. He was seeking absolution without knowing it, and she knew that he would never get it, not from her or anyone else. For she had seen his future. In hellfire.

She said, "I see something else. I see all your cares fall away. I see a large amount of money coming your way. I don't know how, possibly from the sale of your house. I see you in Florida with your friend Mahoney. Now if you will excuse me, Mr. Gilchrist, I have things I must attend to."

She slid sideways out of her chair, away from him.

A look of bewilderment was on his face. "Do you really see all that? That's marvelous . . . I think."

"Come, Mr. Gilchrist, I'm sure you have things to do too."

She escorted him to the front door, speaking reassuringly all the way. When she closed the door she leaned against it and looked at her hands. There were no burn marks on them.

She had seen fire. Raging fire. A person consumed. Many persons consumed. But she didn't see their faces. Perhaps it wasn't Gilchrist at all, not hellfire but earthly fire.

She went to the powder room off her atelier and washed her hands. She peered at herself in the mirror over the sink and shook her head.

What she didn't understand was the initial image that she had seen so clearly. The strange white rose. Her powers had failed her. It was a yellow flower, not white. Oh, dear.

She shrugged philosophically. "That's the way the cookie crumbles," she said to herself.

When Penelope Potter finished her recital, she nodded and said, "Yes, that's it."

Ralph shook himself and said, "What's it?"

She didn't reply, engrossed in her own thoughts.

Ralph said, "It's funny that you used that old expression. There was a great football player named Cookie Gilchrist. You didn't know that, did you? Wonder what ever happened to him."

Penelope Potter stood up. "Come, Mr. Simmons, I'm sure you have things to do."

Ralph laughed. He stood up and hugged her. "You're giving me the bum's rush just as you did to Gilchrist. That's wonderful."

"That's not true at all," she said as she walked with him to the front door.

Ralph said, "Incidentally, Fred Engelhart was one person who actually tried to help the poor bastard when Gilchrist was running up a bill at the club bar that he'll never be able to pay.

"I told Fred to leave the guy alone. When someone's trying to drink himself to death they don't want anyone to butt in. I know, because I was there once. But Fred went over to Gilchrist anyway. This was at the bar, and Gilchrist was alone at the end of the bar nursing his grievances. Fred invited him over to join us. Gilchrist just stared at his drink. Then Fred said, 'Listen, I can use some help in public relations.' And Gilchrist gave him a sloppy grin and said, 'You sure can, Fritz.' That was the end of that."

Ralph gave a helpless gesture. "Just goes to prove that one man's helping hand can be another man's poke in the eye."

Penelope Potter peered at Ralph for a long time. Then she said, "I think he was wrong about the color of the flower."

Ralph had no response to that.

8.

Continuing his circumnavigation of the fire, he walked through torrents descending from the darkened sky. First there was apocalyptic fire, now the gratuitous deluge. Very biblical. The cascade from the sky moved away to douse other trees and houses and save them from the fire. Ralph tasted the water on his face and said, "Yep, that's the bay water I've come to know and love."

The shower revived his flagging energies. He came to his red Skyhawk crouching all by itself at the dock. Sopping. Forlorn looking. He patted the hood and said, "Stand fast, old girl."

A slickered figure came out of the mist trudging north along Shore Road. Ralph caught a flash of the white beard and he called, "Rudi."

Mannheim stopped. He didn't like to be called Rudi—it was a diminishment of his stature—but he tolerated it from Ralph Simmons, knowing it was Ralph's way of being friendly.

"What in God's name are you doing here?" he asked Ralph.

"Visiting my car."

Mannheim shook his head. He didn't understand Ralph's whimsical sense of the ridiculous. "Come on up and dry off, you foolish man," he said.

They trudged along Shore Road together.

"You went down to see the fire?" Ralph said.

Mannheim grunted. "To see if there was anything I could do." He gave a short laugh of self-derision.

Ralph said, "Every firefighter in New York and Long Island is down there. Nothing much they could do either. I heard one of them say, 'Might as well break out the hot dogs and marshmallows.' That's what is called black humor."

"*Schwartzers?*" Mannheim asked in surprise.

Ralph tried to explain what black humor was.

Onlookers had been dispersed by the fallout from the fireboat's water cannon. Ralph and Mannheim were solitary figures in the misty darkness.

Ralph said, "The streetlights are out."

"No electricity," Mannheim said.

Ralph grunted. He really should get back to Lillian, but he had to rest first. Just a few minutes at the Mannheims . . .

The big house off Shore Road wasn't totally dark. Prudence had set a kerosene lamp on the mantel and placed a votive candle near the front door. When Ralph and Mannheim entered, the wind blew the candle out.

Prudence sat in her rocker with a transistor radio to her ear.

"Too much static," she said.

The sight of the Quaker woman holding a transistor radio was out of key. She should be sitting by a spinning wheel or in the kitchen making noodles or churning butter or something.

She said to Mannheim, "Did you see Eric Bushman?"

He said, "We have here a man in desperate need of a sock of schnapps."

"Belt," Ralph said. What he was in desperate need of was a chair to sit in. Dripping bay water, he chose a chair covered in Naugahyde. "Ah-h," he said, as he lowered himself in the chair.

Mannheim brought him a sock of vodka on the rocks, treated himself to a smaller hit and Prudence to a tall tap water. With the windows and doors closed, the room was stuffy, heady with the smell of kerosene and candle wax.

Ralph said, "I should call Lillian and tell her where I am. She might be worrying."

Mannheim said, "Sorry, Ralph, the phones are out too."

"Then I have to make this a short visit." Ralph took a large swig from his glass.

Mannheim stood by the fireplace. The taller Prudence stood by her chair gazing steadily at her husband. She said, "Did you, Rudolf?"

"Did I what? All right, just for a minute. He was there when I passed by. The silly fellow thought they were deliberately trying to give him typhoid or some other terrible disease from the bay water."

"Did you mention Engelhart?"

"Of course not. That's ancient history."

Prudence was silent for a moment; then she said, "You accused Bushman of causing the explosion, didn't you?"

"Certainly not! I didn't accuse, I simply asked, that's all."

"What did he say?"

"Come to think of it, he didn't answer. Just called me names."

"Oh, Rudolf. Stay away from him."

Ralph tried to make sense of the exchange. He pictured in his mind the tall former minor ambassador to minor principalities. What did Eric Bushman have to do with Fred Engelhart?

"If this conversation is private, forgive me," Ralph said. "But what did Bushman have to do with Fred? As far as I know, they never met each other."

Prudence averted her face. "Oh, dear, it appears that I've spoken out of turn." She sat down on the sofa.

Ralph said, "I've always had the feeling that Bushman is holding a watch and giving me three minutes to say something amusing. Then he looks over my shoulder and finds someone else who isn't such a boring clod. He's very polite about it. So when he has a crowd around him and starts telling one of his stories of foreign intrigue, I very politely walk away. I can honestly say that I've never listened to a one of them. I'm sure he hasn't noticed."

"You are wrong, Ralph," Mannheim said. He was standing tall with his back to the fireplace, a psychologist's smile on his face. "Bushman has asked me many times, 'Why doesn't Ralph Simmons listen to my stories?' You have hurt his feelings, Ralph. You shouldn't do that to him." He laughed ponderously at his ponderous joke.

Ralph frowned. "And that's why he goes around blowing up houses?"

"No, no, no, no. We don't like the fellow any more than you do, but we have no reason to believe that he might be so depraved—I mean, the man is in his late seventies. He is an old man."

"A very healthy one," Prudence said.

Ralph peered up at Mannheim holding the high ground as usual. "So I repeat. What the hell did Eric Bushman have to do with Fred? Did they ever meet?"

Mannheim was looking at the wall behind Ralph. "They may have bumped into each other, I don't know. Yes, I seem to remember that one or the other, I forget whether it was Engelhart or Bushman, said that they had bumped into each other."

"You mean literally? Not looking where they're going, and *bam*, oh, I'm so sorry—like that?"

"Possibly." Mannheim shrugged. "I really don't know."

Ralph knew when he was being stonewalled, but this new suggestion that someone may have caused the explosion that killed his friend made him persist. "I understand about the seal of the confessional, or whatever you call the confidentiality between an analyst and his patient, but neither one of these men was a patient of yours, was he?"

Mannheim gazed at him without responding.

Ralph sighed, suddenly acutely aware of his weariness. "Did you know that just a week ago Fred received a flower in the mail? Anonymously, no name, just a card that said *Friedrich*."

Both Mannheims were staring at him.

"A white rose," Ralph went on, "with a piece of red cloth pinned to the center. Fred said that only you knew about the flower, or maybe it was about something else. But he did mention your name."

Mannheim seemed to sag a little. "No. I didn't know about the rose. Strange that he would say my name."

"It doesn't mean anything to you?"

Mannheim slowly shook his head.

"You and Fred Engelhart were brought up in Germany. You knew each other over there, didn't you?"

Mannheim relinquished the high ground. He sat on the sofa beside Prudence. "For a short time," he said. "We were in the army together. The Nazi army. You can understand why we don't like to talk about it. We were children. *German* children. You have to understand that Germany was a patriarchal society, and children were taught to be obedient—"

Prudence said, "You're being defensive, Rudolf. I'm sure Ralph is not sitting in judgment."

Mannheim let out an audible sigh. "No, but I am. It is I who sit in judgment. A fine psychologist. I can't get rid of this feeling of guilt in myself, so how can I help others? I had an alternative, another option, two other options. I could have chosen to go to a concentration camp or to be shot as a traitor. They were choices I never for a minute considered, I didn't know they existed, I merely followed."

Ralph said, "You were drafted. I was too. I was in the army, you were in the army, we survived. What's the big deal?"

Mannheim shook his head. "There's a difference. We could talk about it all night and not get anywhere. Let me just say, if you can understand the human tide of fifteen-year-old Iranians flowing against Iraqi guns, then you can understand the young German soldier at that time. No, that's not exactly right. We weren't that stupidly unaware, we had no Moslem heaven to look forward to. We were just—Wagnerian. Do you see what I mean?"

"I think so," Ralph said. "So you and Fred were in the German army together. Where does Eric Bushman fit in? Are you telling me that Bushman was in the German army too? I thought he was born here, went to Yale and all that."

"That's what he says." Mannheim stood up, his face very pale in the yellow light of the lamp. He glanced at his empty glass as if to indicate that he was going to the kitchen for a refill. He stayed where he was, however. In the silence of the closed-off room, Ralph could hear the distant roar of the fire.

Prudence said, "Rudolf has a friend who's a professor at Yale University, and he checked the records for us. Bushman was never a student there. Not in the twenties, thirties, or forties when he might have been an undergraduate."

Mannheim said, "To be fair, dear, he did get an honorary degree after that Biafra business. I have my own opinion of his heroics there, but that was twenty-five years after the time we're talking about. Ralph, are you ready for another—" he smiled faintly—"sock?"

"No, thanks, Rudi. I really have to be going."

Mannheim sat down without refilling his glass. "You know the slight limp Bushman has?"

"Yeah, an arthritic hip."

"I don't think so," Mannheim said. "Engelhart and I were in an Alpine unit. We had just moved down to the Apennines from the Alps where we were trained in winter warfare. As I say, we were children, we had just turned eighteen. Then, most ingloriously, Engelhart was in a motor accident. Broken skull, broken shoulder. He was taken to the field hospital and disappeared in the red tape of the medical support pipeline.

"The very next day, or maybe it was two days later, a tall lieutenant with a walking cast on his leg arrived at our headquarters asking about a young soldier who may have been on leave in Munich on such-and-such a date, I don't remember the date. And it turned out by the process of elimination that the soldier was Fred Engelhart. But he was now gone.

"The lieutenant questioned everyone in our platoon about the soldier Engelhart. 'Why are you asking these questions?' we said. He didn't tell us. But I learned from our captain later that someone had tried to kill the Nazi Gauleiter of Munich by throwing a grenade at him outside the Fuhrerhaus. Somehow the lieutenant, who was on the Gauleiter's staff, broke his ankle at the same time. I got the impression that he had tussled with this terrible criminal who would do such a thing. So he was late in trying to track the criminal down.

"That lieutenant was polite, soft-spoken, but there was a coldness in him that made me shiver. It was those pale blue eyes, the icy eyes of winter. I have since, an aversion to blue eyes. You will notice that Prudence's eyes are brown. If they had been blue, I don't think I could have married her.

"And he, the lieutenant, had a little notch on the bridge of his nose from an old wound. The notch is still there. Have you ever looked closely at Eric Bushman's nose? You'll see it there. That lieutenant was Eric Bushman."

Ralph rattled his head as an indication of stunned surprise. "But—but where's his accent, Rudi? Both you and Fred have faint German accents. He talks like an Ivy Leaguer."

"Come on, Ralph, haven't you listened to him enough to know that he has the gift of tongues? He boasts about it in his modest way. He speaks most European languages with little or no accent, I'm told, and several African tongues. After the war, *der Lieutnant* Eric Bushman became the most American German of us all. It's a remarkable gift that the U.S. State Department found irresistible."

"Amazing," Ralph said. "He's lived here, how long? Ten years, and nobody's ever said anything about his Nazi background. Surely it must be on record at the State Department; they wouldn't have invented a whole new background for him . . . Or would they?"

"I doubt it," Mannheim said. "But they wouldn't publicize it either. No, it was Bushman himself who made those vague references to a midwestern childhood and the rest."

"Amazing," Ralph said. "So it would seem that young Fred tossed a grenade at a Nazi functionary, Bushman broke his leg trying to stop him and then was given the mission of tracking him down. Forty-five years ago. Do you really believe that after all this time the lieutenant was still tracking down the would-be assassin? That's wild."

"I don't know anything for sure," Mannheim said. "Here's another wild guess for you. I truly believe that Bushman kept track of me. He knew I was a comrade of Fred's for that short period. And I truly believe that he moved here when he retired to be near me on the chance that Engelhart would seek me out at some point—"

"Now you're really stretching it."

Mannheim grimaced. "Maybe. Maybe. Remember what I said about the German character. I got the distinct impression that Gauleiter Giesler was not only a father figure to the lieutenant but something like a Wagnerian god. And the lieutenant was sent on a quest: find the traitorous assassin and bring him to Nazi justice. The quest was never fulfilled. Time means nothing to a god of vengeance. A lifetime, several lifetimes. Honor demands that you complete your solemn mission even if it takes till the end of time . . .

"And then Fred Engelhart arrived."

"Two years ago," Ralph said. "Did he come because of you? Had you kept in touch?"

"No. That you can put down to coincidence. But it's really not such a farfetched one as it might appear. Fred Engelhart was a wealthy inventor, and he was looking for a place in New York City to build his house. And there aren't many areas in the city where a person like Fred would care to live. He ruled out Manhattan. He loved the city, but he wanted to retreat from its neurotic intensity. He looked around in the other boroughs and came to the same conclusion that Prudence and I had come to. Savage Point was the best place in every way.

"He almost didn't come here. You know the deli down near Northern Boulevard? There's a real-estate office two doors away. He was coming out of the real-estate office at the same time I was coming out of the deli. He didn't recognize me, of course—I didn't have a white beard when I was eighteen. But I recognized him. In spite of the disfigurements of time he looked almost exactly the same, the same red hair and homely face.

"I'm afraid it was I who told him about the property on the bluff. If I hadn't, he'd probably have built his house someplace else, and he'd be alive. Another guilt I'm going to have to live with, Ralph."

"Oh, for the love of heaven," Prudence exclaimed.

Ralph glanced at his watch. Mannheim's cadences had almost put him to sleep. He jumped to his feet. "Hey, people, I've got to get back to Lillian."

Moments later the Mannheims were guiding him through the dark front hall.

"One last thing, Rudi," he said. "Where does the white rose come in? What has that to do with the story of Bushman tracking down Fred Engelhart?"

He couldn't make out Mannheim's face in the darkness.

"I'm not sure it has anything to do with the story. Something *did* happen in Munich around that time; I saw a reference to it long after the war was over. Some students started a peace movement called the White Rose. It was immediately crushed, of course, and that's about all I know about it. The Gauleiter dragged a few pitiful people before the People's Court, they were executed, and that was that. Fred was from Munich, but I have no idea whether he was connected to the movement or not."

He opened the door, and the wind blew mist into their faces.

Ralph stood in the doorway. "Fred said you knew about it. So the two of you must have discussed it."

"We may have," Mannheim said. "You'd better hurry or you'll be cut off by the fire. It looks like it will go clear across to Harper's Cove."

Ralph trudged wearily down Shore Road. A word came to his mind: *unbelievable*. Not that Mannheim was a liar, but his story was a mixture of fact and conjecture, mostly conjecture. Too much . . .

A gust of wind hit him. He peered south and saw the living, roiling cloud with interior red and orange lights, a gigantic lantern of hell on a Halloween night in August.

He hastened his pace. He had waited too long. If he was really cut off from home, Lillian would be worried sick. He had to get through.

He turned up Baycrest Road, a safe street several blocks north of the firestorm's path.

Lillian picked up the phone. That crazy nut Ralph had said he was going to the car. The Mannheims lived nearby. She dialed their number. Nothing happened. What she heard was dead air. *Great!* She went to the front door, glared at the monstrous thing that filled the entire northern sky. She shook her fist at it, at the same time assuring herself that Ralph was too smart to let himself get caught up in it.

Suddenly a ghostie was there on the front lawn, a figure in black, pale Halloween lights playing on the white face. "My God, you scared me," she said.

Teddy Thatcher moved closer. "How's—" He cleared his throat. "I was wondering about Eileen. Is she—"

"She's fast asleep. Come on in."

"No, no." He backed away. "I was just wondering. Tell her I asked."

She watched him move back to his own house and disappear. Poor kid, she thought, he's human, after all. Show's you can't tell a book by its cover.

9.

After leaving the Mannheims, Ralph walked through a forest of dripping trees. Weird. What wonders modern man can produce—instant rain forest. There was enough reflected light in the sky that he could make out the silent houses, some dark and haunted, others showing dim flickers of pre-Edison light. He was sleepwalking through a nightmare landscape. The dull roar in his ears was the fire monster three blocks to the south. The denizens of these stately domiciles were down there rubbernecking, grieving for friends, secretly soothed that the terrible happening wasn't happening to them.

He labored uphill to the spine of Savage Point. The socks in his shoes were sopping, bunching, rubbing, causing sores. Soon there would be blisters. He charged on as fast as he could; he had to beat the fire to Harper's Cove.

Topping the ridge, he was startled to see some houses in flames directly ahead of him, two blocks north of the fire's path. This shouldn't be. The wind was steady, pushing the fire in a widening path, but surely not this wide.

He loped forward past untouched houses. He saw that only two houses were involved on the left side of the street. Strangely those on the right side, closer to the advancing holocaust, were not ignited. As he looked, a third house, beyond the first two, began to exude smoke.

He recognized the first house as the run-down derelict that belonged to Todd Gilchrist. It was also the first one beyond the reach of the great stream of water from the fireboat in the bay. It was a goner. The foliage around it was blazing, rose bushes and all. The heat forced him out into the roadway.

He knew from his ramblings that the second house belonged to Kitty the Cat Woman. He never could remember her last name. Her house was not yet as fully involved as Gilchrist's. The front door was open, and black smoke rolled out at the top of the doorway.

Ralph loved the old woman. If she was still in there, he had to do something. He headed toward the front door. Suddenly a red flash filled the entire doorway, and a hulking figure hurtled out, came toward him with flaming clothes. Ralph was momentarily frightened by the apparition and stepped back.

The figure fell on the lawn, with a cry that sounded inhuman.

Ralph rushed to him, yelling, "Roll! Roll over!"

The figure looked like it was swimming, arms flailing.

Ralph reached out with both hands and tried to roll him on the grass. The man's arms impeded the action, and he slid rather than rolled. Ralph kicked him. "Roll, damn it! Put out the fire!"

A few seconds later the flames were out, but the clothing still smoldered. "Take 'em off," he cried. He yanked the shirt off.

The man lay on his back. His face was blackened, either soot-soiled or charred, Ralph didn't know. He recognized Todd Gilchrist. Ralph took off his wet shirt and put it over the pink flesh of Gilchrist's torso, hoping that the moisture would soothe the burned areas.

"Tried to get to her," the man gasped.

"Dear God, is Kitty in there?"

Gilchrist didn't answer.

"Can you walk?" Ralph asked.

What came out of Gilchrist was a whimper.

Ralph could feel his now-naked chest and stomach being singed in the fierce heat radiating from the house. He grabbed Gilchrist by the feet and dragged him across the street. Gilchrist screamed once and tried to wriggle out of Ralph's grasp. He kicked at Ralph, and Ralph dropped the feet. "Stop it, you stupid son of a bitch. Just a little farther now."

He got the man on the lawn of the darkened house across the street.

"Far as I go," he said, wheezing. He plopped down beside the sprawled figure of Gilchrist, trembling, feeling nauseated, all energy drained. Head hanging, saliva dripping from his mouth, he sat there until the panting slowed. Then he glanced at Gilchrist.

The man was looking skyward, his eyes glazed. "Never thought about her," he mumbled. "You're right, Simmons, I'm a no-good prick. Never knew that 'til now. A goddamned, no-good prick. I killed her."

"That's horseshit, Todd," Ralph said. "Nothing you can do about fire."

Gilchrist tried to laugh and became contorted in a coughing fit. "Act of God," he finally managed to say. "A goddamned act of God, right?" And the charred man started to sob.

The sounds were unbearable to Ralph. He used his hands to push himself to his feet. That was when he found out that his hands were burned.

"Going for help," he muttered. He staggered down the street toward Harper's Cove.

Kitty Henderson was badly scratched. She had managed to herd five of the cats into the unfinished basement after she discovered that the kitchen door was blocked by fire. She knew by her labored breathing that the dank area was filling with smoke. She couldn't see a thing.

The small window that she had pried open was shoulder high. There was no possible way that she could get her old body up there and crawl out to safety. But she was determined to save her precious charges.

She crouched beneath the window. "Come here, Snooty," she crooned. "Come here, Mama." She couldn't see the animals but heard their cries and snarls when something hot dropped on them. They raced about erratically. She felt them brush against her legs. "Come here, Mathilda."

She blindly snatched one in her hands. "Oh, it's you, Snooty. Out you go." She shoved the cat out the window to give it a chance to save itself. But the window was on the far side of the house where the wind tossed fragments of fire every which way, and, unfortunately, the cats she managed to toss out found the environment out there more frightening than the darkness of the basement, and they immediately leaped back in.

She knew the cats by feel. "Out you go, Mama. Say a prayer for me." Mama hung on to her arms with her claws and refused to go out. The old woman finally dropped her into the darkness. "At least you had a happy life, darling. May the end be quick."

A light flared in the darkness at the foot of the wooden stairway. It leaped up the stairs spread-eagled in the air, its fur blazing. The screech died abruptly. "Oh, Mama," the old woman wailed.

Blackie went out and stayed out. "Good for you," she called. "You always were the smart one."

She slumped down to the cement floor under the window. Suddenly a cat was on her lap. She pulled her knees up to protect it. She stroked it soothingly. "They say all cats look alike in the dark," she said softly. "That's not true. In the dark you're very handsome. I call you Ugly as a joke. You're really the best-looking cat of them all, do you hear? Go ahead, dig your claws in, I don't mind."

She coughed violently. Ugly tried to jump off her lap, but she clung to him. "No, stay with me," she crooned, petting his lumpy head. "We'll go together. Won't that be nice?" The cat quieted.

As she stroked him, she hummed "Onward Christian Soldiers." "God put you here for a purpose, Ugly dear," she said. "I've always thought it was to make us more human. Does that sound right? Some say it was to keep the rats from taking over, but I don't believe that."

She coughed, and the cat escaped. A moment later he was back. Her speech was coming with more difficulty. "Let's say a prayer for Mr. Gilchrist. Never mind he drank too much and all that. He tried to help us. You heard him up there. Calling to us. I do hope he's all right. Now, say a prayer, okay?"

With her last bit of strength she stood up, clutching Ugly to her chest. She tried to talk, but she didn't know if the words came out. *Mama had the right idea.* She stumbled toward the staircase. *It's possible we'll walk right through the fire. But I don't think so. Maybe if I had called you Shadrach . . . Hang on, I'm afraid I'm going to—"*

Ralph heard the scream from the next block, and a surge of guilt almost knocked him down. She was still alive in the burning house while he was dragging Gilchrist across the street! Then he told himself there was no way he could have saved her. Doggedly putting one foot in front of the other, he made his way down the street to Harper Road bordering the marshy cove.

Here the fire was only a block away, and the road swarmed with firefighters, vehicles, hoses, and burned-out persons standing in statuelike clusters.

He halted a firefighter and told him of the second fire coming down Baycrest Road, the glow of which could now be seen. When Ralph pointed to it, the fireman said, "Better get that hand treated," then raced away to divert some of the men and equipment to the new blaze.

Ralph looked around blearily, saw an EMS ambulance, staggered to it and sat on its front bumper. The throbbing in his hands was more disturbing than the pain. He found that if he held them above his shoulders the throbbing lessened.

A medic saw the half-naked man sitting with his hands up as if ordered to do so by a thug. "What's it with you?" he asked.

Ralph peered at him for a moment, then said, "There's

a badly burned man up there." He described as best he could the place where he had left Gilchrist.

The medic hurried away, came back with an open jar containing a white ointment. "Slap some of this on your hands, it'll help." He disappeared.

Other medics trudged down the road from the fire lugging a stretcher. Ignoring the ambulance, they carried their burden another block north to a helicopter idling on Memorial Field, an open area dedicated to field sports.

Ralph fought an urge to lie down. He slathered some of the ointment on his hands. In doing so, he discovered that the hands were not uniformly burned, the worst burns being in noncallused spots like between fingers. *Hold the medals, fellers, these are two-bit injuries.* His sense of fatigue lessened, and he realized that part of it had been fear that his burns were severe, the old fear of the unknown.

He stood up, surprised that his legs still worked. He limped to Memorial Field, watched the helicopter take off and another land. Steering clear of the landing area, he made his way across the field to the far end where it fell away into the marshy border of the cove. He stared southward into the darkness.

The fire had indeed stopped at Harper Road, beyond which there were no more houses and little foliage to feed it. Nevertheless the view was still awesome. The unrelenting wind continued on across the cove carrying with it dancing fragments of fire—Puffed Rice shot from a cannon, he thought, or a million roman candles shot by a million Romans. Most of the particles lost momentum and dropped into the black marsh and the shallow channels of water; but some had enough propulsion to reach the shore of Great Neck. Flurries of activity over there suggested that firefighters were there to snuff them.

Gritting his teeth, Ralph stepped down into the boggy blackness. He shuddered. "If there are any snakes in here, just stay outa my way, damn it. That goes for rats, too."

Walking was difficult. The unseen, waterlogggged earth underfoot was tufted, so that he went from spongy firmness to ankle-deep ooze. He headed south into the darkness, keeping the great fire on his right, staying as close to the shore as he could. His target was the unfinished back road across the swamp between Savage Point and Little Neck, a sort of extension of Dover Street. Once there, he would be beyond the fire—he hoped—and only a few blocks from home.

He plodded on in a daze, counting his steps then losing count, trying to think of Lillian waiting for him. He couldn't picture her. At one point he laughed uncontrollably at his predicament, all his own fault. Remind me never to do this again, he thought. His shoes were sucked off in the first few minutes, then his socks. The ooze between his toes was a horror, flesh-eating organisms were consuming him. Several times he fell heavily, covering himself with slime.

Sparks fell on him from the sky, but he was so covered with slime that they were immediately extinguished. He wondered if Fred Engelhart was somewhere watching him slop through the mud and laughing at the ridiculous sight. He pictured a disembodied Fred hovering in the sky. Who did it, Fred? You must know by now, so tell me. Was it Bushman? We'll slap his Nazi ass in solitary. If it wasn't Bushman, who? Damn it, who was it? . . . Or was it just an accident, after all?

He was pushing through tall reeds, which lashed at his body. Suddenly he was on asphalt. He was on the back road! "How about that," he said in wonderment.

He gazed up the hill to the end of Dover Street. Another damn hill to climb. Now he was aware how tender his feet were. Each step found a jagged pebble. He became aware that he was sobbing with the pain, and he cursed himself as an old woman. He stopped and mentally apologized to old women the world over. He found that by sliding his feet forward he could avoid some of the sharp objects . . .

Dover Street was crowded with people and equipment. The people stared at the strange apparition, a half-naked man covered with mud shuffling slowly along, mumbling to himself, and they cringed. A few came to him and asked if they could help, and he said in a cracked voice, "No, I'm going home, thank you." To one, he said, "Do you have a pair of shoes?" The person backed away.

The Savage Point volunteer ambulance was there. He sat on its front bumper. After a moment a volunteer was standing in front of him. It was a middle-aged neighbor named Hagedorn. "Oh, hi, Wally," Ralph said. "You really ought to put cushions on these things. They're not much fun to sit on."

The man tried to wipe the mud from Ralph's face and head. "Where are you hurt, Ralph?" he asked.

"Hands and feet. The hands are okay, but do you have an extra pair of shoes? Never got used to going barefoot."

"No shoes, old buddy, but we'll come up with something."

The man went away, and Ralph stared at the ground.

The man came back. "Here, try these on for size," he said. "They're wallets, mine and Jerry's. Genuine cowhide." He taped them, unfolded, to Ralph's feet. "Now stand up and see how they fit. Do they pinch anywhere?"

Ralph stood up. "Perfect," he said.

"Sure you can make it home?"

"Positive. Thanks. Tell Jerry I owe him."

"No problem."

Ralph wobbled as he walked. The wallets were neither long enough nor wide enough to cover the bottoms of his feet, but by stepping carefully he could walk without further injuring his feet. He called back. "Remember. Next time. I take a nine-and-a-half C." He didn't know whether Wally heard him or not.

Downhill toward home. People still stared at him but as an object of curiosity rather than fright. Clopping exhaustedly toward his panting place, his castle, Lillian. His vision blurred.

He bumped into a tall angular woman. "Oops," he said. "Oh, hi, Judy."

Judith the architect stared at him, and said, "What the hell happened to you?"

Ralph looked from her to her husband sitting on the curb, and then over to Center Drive and the still flaming hulk of their house. "God, I'm sorry, kids," he said.

"It's a way of clearing out the junk," she said.

"Where are you staying tonight?"

She said, "Somewhere. We haven't decided."

He looked again at the fire. "Can anything be salvaged?"

"You're kidding," she said.

"In that case you're invited to stay at the world-famous Simmons Hotel, the both of you. Our house is so large we have rooms we haven't been in yet." He patted the bald dome of Judith's husband. "Up, Stanley. If you keep looking at that, you'll get suicidal or cataracts or something. Let's go, son, you're coming to our house."

The man clambered awkwardly to his feet, clutching his manuscript to his chest. He looked dazed.

Ralph put his arm around Judith's shoulder. "I'm not getting fresh, Judy my love," he said. "It's just that I can use a little support, and old Stanley's not up to it. Jesus, you have bony shoulders."

Judith stiffened, then she laughed. "And you are—literally—a filthy old man. Come on, you smelly old goat."

In this fashion they made their way to Ralph and Lillian's house on Dover.

Ralph slept that night on the chaise longue on the screened-in back porch. Not because Lillian was passionately angry with him, which she was, but because the only water in the house was in the bathtub, which she had had the presence of mind to partially fill before the water stopped flowing altogether. Taking a bucket of the water to the back porch and making Ralph strip off the rest of his sodden clothing, she sponge-bathed him, but he still smelled of rotten vegetation. It was he who insisted on sleeping on the porch, covered only by an old sheet.

He fell instantly into a deep sleep. It didn't last long. The roar of the fire had lessened, but the sounds of the fire vehicles were not exactly lulling, and the animals in the backyard necessarily invaded each others' turf causing territorial disputes of high decibel. Raccoon screeched at raccoon in the old swamp maple, shaking the tree to its roots with their physical combat. Then the raccoon who lost the tree fight got in a shouting match with a very vocal cat. Ralph cursed under his breath, rolled over on the chaise and fell to the floor. He climbed back on and slept deeply until the next clarion screech.

Other things disturbed his sleep. His hands and feet nagged him. The wind grew cooler and chilled him until Lillian tiptoed out to him sometime in the night and put a blanket on him. "Mm," he said to her.

He dreamed that he and Lillian were having cocktails in the bell tower of Engelhart's house. Fred said, "There's something I have to tell you," and then he burst into flames. Ralph started to throw his gin and tonic on him but decided it was an awful waste of good gin. He squirmed with a sense of guilt, knowing that he should have put the fire out. A figure was there holding a large flaming match. Ralph lunged for him. The figure disappeared, and Ralph was flying through the air. He was frightened. He didn't like flying. He wanted to go home but didn't know where it was.

Another image. The white rose in the cardboard box. He grabbed it, and thorns pierced his hands.

Gilchrist said— What was it Gilchrist said? . . .

Ralph opened his eyes. It was daylight, and Eileen Engelhart was perched like a cat in the captain's chair staring at him.

II. Rainstorm

10.

Ralph closed his eyes. "There's an old story," he said. "A drunk falls asleep in a cemetery. When he wakes up in the morning, he looks around and says—"

"Uncle Ralph, it's half past nine."

"There's not a soul in sight, all he sees are the gravestones—"

"Uncle Ralph!"

"You're spoiling a good story."

"Okay. So he looks around, and what does he say?"

"He claps his hands and says, 'Judgment Day, and I'm the first one up!'"

"Everybody else has been up for hours. We have to get moving."

"It's not Judgment Day?"

"In a way, Uncle Ralph." Eileen Engelhart stood up, shook his shoulder. "Old Boomer's here, he wants to look at your hands. And the water's come back on."

Ralph creaked to a sitting position. "Damn, I thought I was the first one up." Eileen was clad in one of Lillian's old granny bathrobes. The lovely young face was puffy, all glitter gone except for the eyes, which seemed to flash laser beams. "Do me something, sweetie," he said. "Tell the old quack to come out here. Tell him my muscles are revolting, and that's not the only thing revolting about me."

Eileen mumbled, "You and your dumb jokes," and left.

Dr. Everett Smith, called Boomer because of his loud voice, was a heavyset man with graying blond hair and the bedside manner of Hulk Hogan. He thumped down beside Ralph.

"So you got caught with your hands where they shouldn't be. Cripes, these hands don't look so bad. I've seen hands that were one big blister, looked like boxing gloves. Yours smell like swamp water. Not the best thing for blistered hands, Ralph, no matter what you've heard. This is just a little germicidal stuff—"

The doctor gabbed on in his resounding voice as he ministered to Ralph's wounds. "The feet don't look too bad, mostly scratches, just one little hole here that you've packed full of mud. You'll have to stop playing in mud for a while. Now we'll check the old ticker."

The firemen—there seemed to be hundreds of them—were still there, and the police were there in force to keep the rubbernecks and scavengers away. The wind had lessened in force as if exhausted from its vicious slashings of the night before, and it had at long last shifted from the southwest to the northwest.

Streamlets of smoke still rose from the smoldering pyres and stung the eyes of Ralph Simmons and Eileen Engelhart as they stood on the corner of Savage Point Road and Schmidt's Lane, having gone through backyards to avoid the police blockade.

The view was one of god-forsaken desolation, a miniature middle-class preview of the end of the world by fire. Nothing remained of the Engelhart house. Next to it a brick chimney stood obscenely tall like a giant's middle finger telling all who saw it to go screw. The brick house on the corner still stood, roofless, windowless, and gutted. The scene to the east was more stunning. A rising hillside of blackened rubble, charred tree trunks and, here and there, some hollowed-out brick buildings. Two brick houses with slate roofs appeared to be blackened but intact.

"My father didn't believe in God," Eileen said. "Only the devil."

Ralph glanced at her. The lovely face was set in grim lines, the young body hidden in a floppy black T-shirt and wrap-around skirt that wrapped around too far. Only Lillian's knock-about sneakers fit her. He knew Fred had had an ironic twist of mind and said many things that were not to be taken seriously, but Ralph merely said, "It does look like the work of the devil, doesn't it?"

The radio had given them a preliminary estimate of the fire's toll: thirteen people dead including two firefighters, ninety-seven houses destroyed, damages over a hundred million dollars. No mention of the wounded hands and feet of Ralph Simmons. He kept his hands down by his side despite the throbbing, because he didn't want to look ridiculous. His feet reported no problem, snuggled in sweat socks and sneakers with added footpads. He felt washed-out and depressed. He wanted to go home and close his eyes for a year or two. But Eileen had said, "There are things I can find out, Uncle Ralph, and there are things you can find out. You know how men are. So let's go."

By hand and by bulldozer firemen were clearing the debris from Savage Point Road, opening a path to stranded householders and fire vehicles trapped to the north of the devastation. New York Telephone and Con Edison workers were standing by to restore connections.

A fireman came back from the labor, and Eileen stopped him. "Who's in charge?" she asked.

He was a young man. "What do you want to know, doll?" he asked.

She turned on the smile that she knew melted the hearts of men. "Who's in charge?"

"It's a good question," the young man said. "The police are trying to horn in, but I think it's still our show. Come on, I'll take you to him. Do you live near here?"

She said, "Come on, Uncle Ralph."

The first official was too busy to talk to them. He shunted them to an assistant, who pointed to two other men, an older one in charge of rescue and one in charge of investigation.

Rescue at this stage meant the retrieving of dead bodies. Ralph said to the man, "There was a body in the first house."

The man shuffled some papers. "Yes, the Engelman house."

"Engelhart," Ralph said. "Fred Engelhart."

The man looked at him suspiciously. "You sure?"

"Yes. This young lady is Eileen Engelhart. She lived there."

"We didn't find any Fred Engelhart in there."

"I know. He's in the morgue at Long Island Jewish Hospital. He was thrown clear."

"Are you getting this, Clifford?" Rescue said to a man with a clipboard who stood beside him.

"Yes, sir."

Ralph said, "There was another person in the Engelhart house. What happened to her?"

"There was? What's her name?"

"Angel Jones."

"Are you a relative?"

"Angel Jones was this young lady's stepmother."

"Mrs. Engelman?"

"Engelhart. No, she was Angel Jones. She kept her own name because she was an actress."

"Oh-h," the man said, nodding. "That explains it."

He had a whispered conversation with his assistant; then he put an arm around Ralph's shoulder and took him aside. "She's dead," he told Ralph in a low voice, presumably to keep the sad news from the bereaved stepdaughter.

"Where is she?" Ralph asked. "We want to make arrangements."

"Well, that's kind of a sticky thing." The man lowered his voice still further. "She wasn't in one piece, if you know what I mean. We found what you might call parts of her all over the place. Lord knows if we got all of her."

"I understand. Where are her—remains?"

"Body bag. Down at the church hall. We're using that as a temporary morgue."

"How is it tagged?"

The man called out, "How's it tagged, Clifford?"

"Jane Doe—House One."

Ralph somberly thanked the two of them.

He went to Eileen and said, "Since I can't hug you, you gotta hug me, honey." He used his arm to hug her shoulder. "She's down at the church hall."

She said hesitantly, "Uncle Ralph, will you—?"

"Did she have any relatives?"

"Only us."

"I'll go call Greaney." Bill Greaney, a neighbor who ran a funeral home in Little Neck, was the unofficial undertaker of Savage Point.

"Stay with me," she said, clutching his arm.

The man who was in charge of investigation stood at the end of Schmidt's Lane watching a half dozen men sift through the rubble of the Engelhart house. He was a stocky man with the face of a bloodhound.

Eileen tugged at his sleeve. "Have you found it?" she asked.

He said, "Go away, miss. You're not supposed to be here."

She said, "It's my house. Have you found what caused the explosion?"

He pointed to a man wielding what looked like a metal garden rake. "See that, miss? That's a fine-tooth comb. It'll be days before we know anything. Tell me this, were there any propane tanks in there? A neighbor says the crazy owner had propane in there."

"The crazy owner was my father."

"Sorry. I'm only quoting the neighbor. Were there propane tanks in there?"

"No."

"Any other hazardous material?"

"What's your name?"

"Novak. Why?"

"It wasn't an accident, Mr. Novak. It was murder. My father was murdered. Someone put a bomb or something in there and killed my father."

"Who might that someone be? Did he have enemies?"

"Stupid people didn't understand him. He frightened them."

"A lot of people?"

"Yes."

The man nodded. "I get the picture. A stupid person. Now, if you'll just let us get on with our work—"

Ralph Simmons said, "What do you think happened, Mr. Novak? What does it look like?"

The bloodhound scowled at him. "Most of the time it's hazmat. Hazardous material. Sometimes it's not. Sometimes we never find out. We'll just have to see what turns up." He moved away from them, spoke to a man in a bulldozer that was standing by.

Eileen said, "He thinks I'm crazy."

"It doesn't matter," Ralph said. "He'll be honest about what he finds. There are things we have to do back home, sweetie. Nothing more we can do here."

Reluctantly they went home, where Ralph made arrangements for two funerals.

After the firemen checked out her house, Penelope Potter was permitted to reenter it with her husband. The damp reek of charred wood was everywhere. She guided the tall, spare frame of her husband to his seat at his desk. "You really should go to bed," she said.

He waggled a finger, made a sound in his throat.

"Breakfast then. I'll see if the milk is still fresh in the refrigerator. Henrietta bought it only yesterday."

She took his lack of response as assent.

She went to the hall, headed for the kitchen. Henrietta came out of Penelope's study at the end of the hall and stood in the doorway as if barring entry.

"Don't go in there, Miss Potter," Henrietta said.

"Whyever not? Is there something wrong in there?"
"It's the—" Henrietta began to weep.
"Oh, for pity sake, it can't be all that bad."

Penelope bustled into the room and looked around. The reek was here too, mixed with a sharper odor that she couldn't identify. Everything seemed in order, the conversation area, the paneled walls, her desk by the window. The illumination from the window was subtly different, somehow both darker and brighter with a suggestion of red that hadn't been there before.

She looked at the window, the great stained-glass window that depicted the Blessed Virgin's—Penelope Potter's?—assumption to heaven. It was now a descent into hell. The glass was bubbled, the sunny landscape beneath the lady's feet was now an unrecognizable jumble of colors, with the red of the sun predominating. To Penelope's horror-struck eyes, it was a landscape of fire. And the figure of the lady was partially melted, sinking, the beatific visage now one of anguish, a soul in torment.

She stared at the grotesque scene, felt her own face twist into a likeness of the Virgin's. She dropped to her knees.

Henrietta said, "What is it, Miss Potter?"

Penelope heard the question, and the answer came together piecemeal in her mind. This is an important message, she thought, if I can only understand it. Clearly I'm being brought down, I'm in danger of hellfire, my feet are uncomfortably hot. In my pride, I identified with the Virgin, is that it? Sin of pride. Blasphemy. Married to St. Joseph. I thought of him as St. Joseph, a real-estate manipulator who never did any carpentry work in his life.

She imagined she covered her face with her hands in self-abasement, but she didn't. She continued to stare at the surreal scene. Henrietta said, "Miss Potter," but Penelope didn't hear her.

She saw the rose blossom from the pink of the lady's gown. Moreover, she now saw that the heat had done strange things to the brown cross that loomed above the fiery landscape. The ends of the crossbar had melted and the color had run, so that in her mind the cross was no longer a cross but the beginning of a swastika. She felt greatly troubled. The past is not dead and buried, after all; it wells up into the present like toxic liquid from an illegal dumping. The evil that men do lives after them, and the evil has oozed up into Savage Point and has brought this devastation.

Is this the message? Or am I straining to find a message where there isn't one? She suddenly felt very old. "Help me up, Henrietta," she said. "I believe I'll rest for a while."

St. Joseph went without breakfast, but he wasn't aware of it. He had died at his desk—in the saddle, so to speak.

The problem of the dead was now in the hands of Bill Greaney, the undertaker. Ralph Simmons and Eileen Engelhart had nothing to do for the rest of the day. Nothing urgent, that is.

Ralph tried to snooze on the back porch, but the southwest wind was still raging through his mind and throwing his thoughts about like Dorothy's tornado: Fred Engelhart floated by, shouting soundlessly; an army sergeant roared, "Simmons!" Ralph's muscles twitched.

Teddy Thatcher was with Eileen in the backyard. The raccoons and other suburban wildlife had disappeared. She said, "This waiting is the pits. I'm tied down. I don't have any clothes. Or money. Even my car, it was there somewhere in the fire, and I didn't see it. I think I'm coming apart."

He tentatively put his arm around her shoulders. He said, "We've got money to burn, my mother and I. It's yours—"

She said, "Do you have a knife?"

"A Swiss Army knife. Why?"

"Let's play mumbletypeg."

"What the devil is mumbletypeg?"

"It's a game Uncle Ralph taught me. Come on, I'll show you."

He said, "I don't like the look in your eyes."
She held out her hand.
She took the knife, opened the blade, felt its edge. "Wow, you keep it sharp."
She led him to a patch of bare earth near the house, made a large circle in the earth with the knife. "Now you do this." She crouched, and with a snap of her wrist she flipped the knife and sent the blade, point first, into the ground inside the circle. "You see the way the knife is facing. You cut a line in that direction, and this part of the pie is mine. Now it's your turn."
"It's not very good for the knife, is it?" he said.
"Shoot."
He failed to stick the blade in the earth. On her second flip, she stood and sent the blade deep into the ground.

Ralph was awakened by Teddy saying loudly, "Cool it off, love, you're going to hurt yourself!"
Ralph opened his eyes and saw Eileen kneeling on the ground and, holding the knife in both hands, plunging it again and again into the ground as if in a murderous rage.
He and Teddy were able to wrest the knife from her hands and guide her onto the porch, where she sank into a chair and sobbed quietly.
Teddy said, "My poor knife."
Marlene Thatcher was standing in her yard on the other side of the hedge, watching. Ralph said to Teddy, "I think your momma wants you."
She called to Ralph, "Is there anything I can do, Mr. Simmons? I do so want to be a good neighbor." The voice was graciously modulated yet strangely detached, as if she were commenting on the weather. Then she did comment: "It looks like we're in for a bit of rain."
Ralph ambled to the hedge. "If you're on speaking terms with God," he said, "tell Him He's too damn late."
"Eileen's taking it badly, isn't she?"
"Nothing unusual. It's the way daughters act."

"Is Teddy being of help? He really should study before he goes back to university. He's studying engineering, you know. It was what his father studied although he never practiced it, poor dear. Managing the properties took up all his time. So if Teddy is just getting in the way—"

Ralph turned and called, "Hey, Ted, your momma wants you."

After a minute Teddy came slowly across the yard and went through the hedge. The open knife was still in his hand. He followed his mother into the house.

Ralph grimaced, wondering why he was taking out his frustrations on the English kid.

11.

That morning the newspaper reporters and TV crews found out where the eccentric inventor's daughter was staying. They came around the side of the house to the backyard, where Ralph confronted them.

"Whoa, hold it, for God's sake. You're trampling my crabgrass. What do you expect Miss Engelhart to say? She is devastated by the loss of her father. All her personal possessions went up in the fire. She herself was slightly burned trying to rescue him—"

"Tell us about that," someone said.

"Not yet, please. She's in borrowed clothes, and she needs time to get herself together—"

"Tell us about the explosion."

"She doesn't know anything about it. She was out in the middle of the bay—"

"Why did her father keep propane in the house?"

"He didn't," Ralph said. "Whatever caused the explosion, it wasn't—"

"It was murder!" Eileen called from the screened porch. "Somebody murdered my father!"

"Come on out here, Miss Engelhart."

"Did she say murder?"

"Tell us who did it. We're your friends." The pack crowded toward the porch. A TV reporter was holding a microphone through a hole in the screening.

Ralph stood in front of the porch doorway. "That's enough, damn it. Come back around five. Maybe she'll have something to say by then." He was humiliated that the whole country was going to see the rusted screening of his back porch. He put his arm around Eileen and led her into the house.

An hour later Ralph was able to go up Savage Point Road to the dock and get his car. Then he and Lillian, having gotten sizes from Eileen, drove to Stern's and bought some basic articles of clothing. They made Eileen stay home, telling her that the reporters would follow her all over the store. "Even into the underwear department," Lillian had said.

Eileen said sulkily, "Who cares?" But she let Ralph and Lillian do the buying for her.

Prudence Mannheim stood on the second-floor deck and peered across the bay. Clouds were tumbling down from the north, washing the blue from the bay waters, leaving a gray residue. The wind was indecisive, trying first one direction then another. With her strong pioneer's face and modest colonial dress, she might have reminded an observer of a whaler's wife on a widow's walk searching the sea for a sail.

"Weather's changing," she said.

Rudolf Mannheim stood in the doorway behind her, a step above her. "I didn't tell Simmons the truth," he said, more to himself than to her.

"You didn't lie," she said.

"Withholding is a form of lying," he said in a dull voice. "The question is, not why I lied but why I told him anything at all. It was very unprofessional."

She turned to look at him. "I didn't know you were a professional psychologist in 1943," she said.

"Of course, I wasn't."

"Then professional ethics have nothing to do with it, do they? You were an eighteen-year-old boy—"

"A Hitler youth."

"Everybody was at the time. Stop picking at old scabs,

Rudolf, it's morbid. We need a few things from the market. Shall we go now or later?"

"Neatly put, my dear," he said with a faint smile. "The preemptive option, which is no choice at all. And a change of subject, to boot. Wonderful."

"I thought you'd like that," she said.

"Very well. I need the exercise. I'll walk down."

"I'll go with you."

He turned back into the house. "No, just give me the list. Someone should stay here in case."

"In case of what?"

"Lord knows. Make it a short list."

She followed him into the house. "It'll probably rain before you get back."

"Let it."

A few minutes later she handed him the list. "Are you going to speak to the police about Eric Bushman?" she asked.

"I don't know."

She said, "Rudolf." She waited until his eyes met hers. "He's your scab. Leave him alone."

"I have no intention of going near him."

She watched him march down Shore Road until he disappeared around the bend.

Detective Lieutenant Joseph Carbine of the New York Police Department was standing in the Simmons living room. His tall, lean body was garbed in a light gray suit, white shirt, blue tie. The only things that tabbed him a policeman and not a yuppie were the sturdy Knapp shoes on his feet. A uniformed cop stood near the door. Lillian Simmons thought the lieutenant looked like a Latin movie star.

Eileen came down the stairs dressed in blue jeans and sneakers, having refused to wear the nice navy dress that Lillian had bought her for the wake. With the natural grace of youth she brought elegance to the simple garb. Teddy Thatcher stood at the foot of the stairs as stiff and unobtrusive as a newel post. Judith the architect and her husband were standing by the piano.

Carbine said, "I'd really like to talk to you one at a time."

Ralph said, "If you'll get rid of the mob in the yard, you could use the back porch."

Lillian said, "Why don't we all sit down, then it won't seem so crowded."

Everyone found a seat except the cop at the door. Carbine sat on the edge of a chair. Eileen sat erect on the sofa. Carbine said to her gravely, "Miss Engelhart, you have twice asserted that your father was murdered. On what facts do you base that claim?"

"He just was, that's all," she said. "He had nothing that would go off by itself, none of that dumb propane. So it had to come from outside."

The detective continued to gaze at her.

She said angrily, "It stands to reason, doesn't it? If he didn't do it, then somebody else did."

"Like who?"

"Like a lot of people—"

Ralph said, "Did they find anything at the site?"

Carbine switched his gaze to Ralph.

Ralph said, "Any evidence of the explosive that was used, or a detonator, or whatever?"

Carbine said, "Do you have any idea of what happens to a detonator when it sets off a charge? It's blown to bits."

"But not completely destroyed," Ralph said. "There must be metallic fragments . . . or is everything plastic these days?"

"It seems that way, doesn't it?" Carbine turned back to Eileen. "Since this is all speculation, who—?"

Ralph persisted. "Have they found anything like that yet?"

Carbine said, "I'm talking to Miss Engelhart."

She said, "Why don't you answer Uncle Ralph's question? I have a right to know what they found."

Ralph said, "Have they ruled out gasoline? You could probably smell that. Or a break in the gas line?"

Carbine said coldly, "They haven't ruled out anything. The probability is that it wasn't gas or gasoline.

But there are so many fragments, and each has to be analyzed—"

"But there may have been a detonator?"

Carbine shrugged. "It's possible." He smiled faintly. "Who's doing the investigating here, Uncle Ralph—you or me?"

Ralph shrank back in his chair. "Sorry."

"Do all the pretty young girls in Savage Point call you Uncle Ralph? I remember another young lady—"

Lillian said, "Yeah, how about that?"

Ralph said uncomfortably, "There are worse things to be called . . . So there probably was a detonator?"

Eileen said, "I knew it! Good going, Uncle Ralph."

Carbine stared both of them down.

"I want to find out about Mr. Engelhart," he said. "I'll start with Miss Engelhart."

For the next fifteen minutes he gathered what facts he could from the dead man's daughter. Ralph was surprised at how little she knew about her father: they had lived at several different places in Greenwich Village, he had taken her to the Bronx Zoo, to the theater, to Belmont race track, Yankee Stadium, many art exhibits because she had shown interest in art and had in fact determined to become a sculptor; all in all, a pretty good father-daughter relationship.

When the subject turned to Fred's early days in Germany, about which Eileen knew very little, Ralph's thoughts went back to the white rose and to Rudolf Mannheim's recitation of the night before. He was annoyed to find that his memory was hazy. If he tried to tell the tale to the police detective, it would sound weak and unbelievable. He said, "There's a man here, Lieutenant, who was in the German army with Fred Engelhart. It might be a good idea to talk to him." He gave him Mannheim's name and address.

Carbine said, "Any other suggestions?"

Ralph said, "For what it's worth," and told him about the white rose that had come in the mail. "Mannheim might know something about that."

"A white rose," Carbine said without expression. He wrote it down in his pad. "Anything else?"

Judith the architect said, "You should know about that house of his, officer."

"What about the house?"

"It was an affront to the whole area. An abomination."

Carbine nodded. "I'm told the neighbors resented it. Did they want to demolish it?"

"Not actually," she said. "But if it happened to disappear, they wouldn't have mourned its loss."

"I see," Carbine said. "A white rose and a house that was an abomination. Did *you* want to destroy it, ma'am?"

"I certainly did. But if you're asking if I actually blew it up with dynamite or plastique or whatever, the answer is no. I only do things like that in my mind, not in the field."

Carbine said, "It's interesting that you mention plastique. May I ask where you were when the explosion occurred?"

Judith grinned broadly. "Fantastic," she said. "Actually we were all on Rudolf Mannheim's boat out in the middle of the bay." She looked around. "In fact, everybody here was there."

Carbine said, "Who else was on the boat?"

"Would you believe a judge?" Judith said. "Lovely. I have a civil court judge as my alibi!"

Carbine stolidly wrote down the names of everyone who had been on the boat. Then he said, "Tell me about this man Gilchrist. Todd Gilchrist."

"Oh, come on!" Ralph said. "The man was no friend of Fred's, but I'm sure he had nothing to do with the explosion."

"He was seen walking away from the scene."

"He was?" Ralph said in surprise. "I can't believe it. In my mind the miserable bastard is a hero. He tried to save his neighbor, the Cat Woman, and wound up with some terrible burns." He held up his own burned hands. "I had to pull him out of the way."

Carbine raised his eyebrows. "You're the one. You didn't give your name."

Ralph shrugged. "The poor guy didn't murder anybody."

"Oh, he's a murderer all right," Carbine said. He flipped a page in his pad. "Mr. Gilchrist was responsible for the death of the neighbor you say he tried to save. Catherine Henderson."

"You mean because he started the fire at Engelhart's house? You have no proof of that, do you?"

"No," Carbine said. "But he was an arsonist just the same. He set fire to his own house, it was an amateurish job, and it spread to the Henderson house and about ten others. Henderson was the only death."

"Bull, his house was caught in the fire like everyone else's."

Carbine shook his head. "Take my word for it. If he pulls through, he's going to be charged with murder. My only question is, did he set just the one fire or two? Tell me about him and Mr. Engelhart."

Ralph continued to insist that Gilchrist had nothing to do with Fred Engelhart's death. "What did he have to gain? Let's get on to something else."

Carbine was regarding him with an amused smile. "I've seen this before, Mr. Simmons. When you save a man's life, you feel responsible for him, and you want to continue to help him. If Gilchrist pulls through, I bet you'll get a lawyer to defend him—"

"Speaking of lawyers," Ralph said, standing up. "Eileen needs one to handle the estate and cut through all the crap." He turned to Eileen. "You've met Eddie Epstein, the guy with the Mount Rushmore face and the curly red hair. Is he okay with you?"

"Whatever you say, Uncle Ralph," she said.

Carbine said, "Sit down, Uncle Ralph, I'm not through. Now, about Gilchrist."

And so the interrogation went on, and Ralph fumed. He was angry at Carbine for so glibly explaining his defense of Gilchrist. What a lot of bullshit.

And for the first time in more than two months there was rain in Savage Point. Thunder rattled the house, and heavy rain drummed on the roof of the back porch. It quickly cleared the backyard of besieging journalists.

At long last the detective and his blue-coated sentinel departed. No one spoke for several minutes as tensions lessened. The sound of the rain was soothing.

Eileen peered up at Ralph. "What do you think?"

Ralph said, "I've met him before. He's a pretty sharp guy."

She jumped to her feet. "I want to walk in the rain!" She was looking at Ralph.

He said, "You walk alone, sweetie. I'm not going out in that."

Suddenly Ted Thatcher was beside her. "I'll go with you, love. I need the air."

Lillian found rain gear for them, and the two young people plunged out the front door.

Then she and Ralph moved to the back porch to watch the downpour. "Isn't it glorious!" she said.

Tunnel vision. Eileen huddled in Lillian's poncho and looked straight ahead as she and Ted plodded down Dover Street. Even so, raindrops swooped under the hood and pelted her lashes. She steered him across somebody's lawn to the temporary opening in the brush made by the firemen.

He said, "I don't think this is a good idea."

She pushed through the opening, and he followed her.

She stood on her father's land two paces from the spot where his body had lain. It seemed to her that all sound ceased and the raindrops were motionless in the air; her father's spirit was everywhere, peaceful and yet restless. She felt that she was communicating with him. She did something she hadn't done in years. She blessed herself.

Someone nudged her arm. Teddy Thatcher. She had forgotten he was there. He gestured toward a figure in black standing in Schmidt's Lane.

"He's praying," Teddy muttered.

Eileen recognized Pastor Karl of the Savage Point

Church. She went to him. "Were you praying for my father?" she asked.

"I hope you don't mind," the man said, fixing her with his pale blue, watery eyes. "All people are the children of God." He was bare-headed, and rain streamed down his face. His yellow hair was pasted to his skull.

She said, "Thank you, Pastor. Why don't you wear a hat?"

"I guess I forgot," the man said. "I came and saw this terrible scene, and I thought of Saint Matthew's words, *the abomination of desolation*, and I thought they fit, even though he was talking about idolatry. There's much of that going around. I decided to go to each house in which there was death, regardless of their faith, and pray for their souls. This was the first house, I was starting here. What was your father's name?"

"Fred Engelhart." She spelled it out. "He wasn't alone."

"Oh, dear, I didn't know that. And who was the other person?"

Eileen told him. She added, "They were murdered."

The man looked shocked. "Murdered," he said, "murdered." He frowned, and it was obvious he was trying to think of a prayer that was applicable to the repose of souls who were the victims of murder. "Oh, my, if what you say is correct, then everyone else was murdered too. For if a man commits a work of the devil, he is responsible for all the consequences of the act. I greatly fear that man is beyond redemption. A mass killer like that can never possibly atone—"

"Wait a minute, Pastor." Teddy had huddled alongside Eileen in bored silence. Now he said, "The Anglican Church teaches that no man is beyond redemption—"

"Well, theoretically, young man, but—"

"Not only that, sir, aren't you judging and condemning someone without knowing his motivation? You drop a bomb on a city and kill a thousand people, are you a mass murderer? But suppose you do it in a time of war—"

"You sound like a seminarian, young man. You raise

theoretical questions which are important but not in a rainstorm. Are you saying that there could be a justification for the act of murdering this young lady's father? If there is a war being waged, I am not aware of it. I would be delighted to discuss these things with you some other time. You're right, young lady, I should have worn a hat. I must do this quickly, and then return for a more proper, er, prayer session."

Eileen tugged Teddy away. They trudged up the lane, turned up the reopened roadway toward the point.

"What came over you?" she asked.

He said miserably, "I made an arse, a jackass of myself, didn't I? It's just that I can't abide a person who speaks with such certainty about something he knows nothing about. I shouldn't have opened my trap."

"My father always said, Never argue with a priest or your mother. They have all the answers directly from God, and there's no way you can win."

"But that sanctimonious sod—"

"Shut up, Teddy. I thought it was nice of the pastor to pray for Dad. And I want you to pray for him too, damn it."

They sloshed up Shore Road through the pelting rain.

He said, "Let me know when you're ready to turn back."

"You can't just turn back. You have to get somewhere before you can turn back."

"Where is somewhere, may I ask?"

"The dock. That's somewhere. I'll be tired by then."

At the dock they paused and viewed the stormy bay. The air was so opaque with rain that they could scarcely see the end of the dock. Something moved out there, deceptive to the eye, for whole air masses were moving. They started their return trek, with the wind now at their backs.

Eileen peered once again at the dock. Where there had seemed to be two shapes out there, there was now one. She was sure it was a person. She wondered who in his right mind would venture out on a windswept dock in a heavy downpour. Her curiosity made her halt.

"There's somebody out there," she said, pulling the reluctant Teddy through the gateway to the dock.

The blurry figure had its back turned toward them and seemed to be staring fixedly into the turbulent water.

Teddy said, "Maybe the lunatic is fishing. I've heard that it's a good time to go fishing."

The distant figure turned abruptly, picked up a shopping bag, and came toward them at a quick pace, head down.

When the figure was nearly upon them, Eileen called out, "What's up, Doc?"

The head snapped up. From under his rain hat, Rudolf Mannheim gazed at her in surprise. "My God, you scared me," he said.

To Eileen, the look on his streaming, whiskered face was not surprise. It was something like horror.

12.

"But what was Doc Mannheim doing out there?" Eileen asked Ralph.

They were on the back porch. The rain had stopped, the air was cool, and they were sipping hot chocolate.

"What did he say?" Ralph asked.

"A couple of things. He liked to go out there when no one else was around, I don't know, like, to commune with the spirit of the sea or something, or to communicate with himself, something like that. Then he said he wanted to see if the fireboat had done any damage to the dock. Also to make sure the float hadn't torn loose in the storm. Take your pick."

"All of the above," Ralph said. "Psychologists are always in there thinking, plugging away, they can't help themselves. If you say to them, just as an example, 'I don't like pistachio ice cream,' they say, 'Mm, that's very interesting.' And they want to know if it's the color you can't stand, or the texture, or the flavor, until you have to tell them to get off your case. They're probably doing it to themselves all the time too. Personally, I think it's funny."

"But he was carrying a bag of groceries that was filled with water. That's not funny, it's nutty."

"That, too," Ralph said.

* * *

Prudence Mannheim was on the phone in the kitchen when her husband dragged himself in out of the slackening rain. She had been calling all the organizations she could think of to volunteer her services to help neighbors victimized by the fire, and had received essentially the same answer from each: the middle-class homeless were taking care of themselves very nicely, thank you.

She hung up and peered at her bedraggled husband, then at the plastic shopping bag that he held by only one loop. She took it from him and put it in the sink.

Still in his slicker, he slumped into a chair, dripping rainwater on the floor. She said, "Something happened." She unsnapped the coat and managed to get it off him along with his hat. She tossed the garments on the floor of the extension in back of the kitchen. Then she wiped his face with a kitchen towel, put some water on the stove to heat.

"You'll have some tea in a moment," she said, sitting on another chair. "What happened, Rudolf?"

His eyes focused on her, and the strange look faded away. "Nothing, my dear," he said. "I suddenly realize I'm getting old." His eyes slipped away from her.

Over the next half hour, while she poured tea for the two of them and they sat with their cups over the kitchen table, she gently but persistently kept at him. "You look like you've seen a ghost," she said. "Something happened, didn't it?" And he kept evading her. Then she said, "You saw Eric Bushman, didn't you?"

"No!" he shouted. Clenched fists thumped on the table, rattling the cups. Then he sort of shriveled and said, "Yes ... Yes, I saw Bushman. It was—it was—I can't believe it happened." He covered his face with his hands.

Little by little, she drew the story from him.

Rudolf Mannheim was in there thinking, plugging away. He couldn't help it, it was what he did. The wind hastened his steps as he walked briskly down Shore Road toward the market near the railroad station. Instead of continuing to where Shore Road curved and terminated at Savage Point Road, he veered up Dock Lane to avoid going past Bushman's house.

Going through the cleared segment of the road, he was shocked at the extent of the devastation. His depression deepened; it was the ruins of World War II all over again. His eyes were drawn to the remnants of Fred Engelhart's house, and his old uneasiness returned. Engelhart had always disturbed him even when they were young soldiers together in the Alps of Bavaria and the Apennines of Italy: he had no insight into his friend's mind, had found no predictability in his actions. This was still true, the practicing psychologist baffled by the eccentric inventor. And there was always the burden of guilt heavy on his shoulders.

He shrugged. No, by God in Heaven, the guilt was Bushman's, not his! The tall, overbearing lieutenant had picked out the one soldier who had been friendly with the young bomb thrower from Munich. The lieutenant had taken the timid boy into a woodshed where they were alone. Mannheim was told to sit on a chopping block; the lieutenant stood over him. The lieutenant called him "Rudi," but the patronizing tone made him feel like a naughty boy called before the headmaster. Instead of a switch, however, this headmaster had an ax in one hand while the other hand rested on the Luger holstered on his hip.

No threat was uttered, but the boy was intelligent, he knew his life was on the line. He told the lieutenant everything he knew about his friend Friedrich. Since Engelhart's personnel file had gone with him to the field hospital and would accompany him through the medical evacuation system, the only information the lieutenant had to go on came from the quaking Mannheim.

The rain came before Mannheim reached the market. Trudging through it, he squirmed mentally trying to blot out the indelible memory—he eagerly thrusting the photograph of Friedrich at the lieutenant. It was a photo of the two of them, Rudolf and Friedrich, in an Alpen scene, snapped by a fellow soldier with a new Leica.

The lieutenant had said, "Thank you, Rudi, I never did get a good look at the cowardly fellow. His back was turned to me. I was looking at the Gauleiter coming out of the Fuhrerhaus, just as he was. There were a number of people around him. I saw him reach into his bag and take out the damned *bomba a mano*. His movement was quick, and if I weren't quicker he would have blown my leader to bits. I want you to tell me why he would do such an insane thing. I jumped on him just as he was tossing it and fortunately saved my leader's life. But the slimy fellow got away. Somehow I was thrust over his shoulder and down the stone steps. That's when I got this." He took his hand off the gun and tapped his plaster cast.

"As I lay there in shock, I was aware the man stood erect and stared for many seconds at the terrible scene he had caused before he turned and scurried away like an animal. But I still didn't get a good look at his face. So thank you, my dear Rudi, for showing me the face of the madman. May I keep this? You'll be doing your fatherland a service."

"Yes, keep it, keep it," said the young soldier Mannheim.

"Now tell me about his connection with the White Rose traitors."

Mannheim stammered that he knew nothing about any white rose.

The lieutenant unsnapped the holster. "Don't disappoint me, Rudi. Are you saying that he never told you of his association with Hans and Sophie Scholl? You were his best friend. Of course, he told you."

"Yes, of course, he did," Mannheim said.

The lieutenant nodded. "We thought we had eliminated all the pitiful conspirators in the student revolt, but we obviously missed a few, didn't we? Your friend was deluded, Rudi. He apparently blamed the Gauleiter for their deaths when it was actually the president of the People's Court who condemned them.

"Now tell me about this professor of philosophy, Kurt Huber. I think we'll find that your redheaded friend—I can't tell from this photograph, but I did observe that the grenade thrower had red hair—I think we'll find that young Friedrich was a student of the traitorous professor."

"Yes," Mannheim said. "Now that I think about it, he did mention a Professor Huber."

"I thought so," the lieutenant said. "You'll be happy to learn that the good professor was hanged right after his disciples Hans and Sophie and the other misguided students. And that was the end of the White Rose."

"Please, Herr Lieutenant, I don't understand this white rose," Mannheim said. "Would it be possible for you to—"

The lieutenant frowned, then cleared his throat. "There are always some rotten apples, Rudi," he said. "Some of our pampered students—very few, thank God—quaked in their boots when they heard of our little setback at Stalingrad, and they started a movement to turn out the Fuhrer and end the war. Can you imagine, they were revolting against the Fuhrer! It's pitiful, really. They exchanged letters with students at other universities. These were called the 'White Rose letters.' Stupid. The whole thing was very stupid and died of its own stupidity. But obviously one of the stupid persons got away. So tell me more about him. Tell me about his family, his momma and his poppa. They lived in Munich, I take it."

Young Private Mannheim had no more facts to tell, but the lieutenant wasn't content with that. So the private launched into fiction featuring the evil professor and vague misdoings in the Engelhart household in Munich. He had to be circumspect to avoid trapping himself in a conspiracy he had never heard of before, a possibly fictitious conspiracy. He invented stories with an innocent surface and let the lieutenant imbue them with evil meaning. It would have been ironic indeed to lie himself into a nonexistent conspiracy and be executed for it.

Many decades later, in Savage Point on the edge of New York City, he learned from Fred that his parents and younger brother had died at Buchenwald. He had no way of knowing whether his carefully concocted fictions, manufactured in an Italian woodshed to save his own neck, had anything to do with the fate of Fred's family in a German concentration camp. Thus his guilt could never be justified and possibly atoned, nor dismissed as baseless. It was just there.

He huddled in his slicker and groaned.

Returning from the market, he had to slog into the wind-driven rain. In addition to basic things like milk and rolls that were on Prudence's list, he had bought her a special treat that was now in the shopping bag, a slice of the market's own home-made poundcake. He forced his mind to anticipate her delight and to concentrate on the feel of the rain in his face and the extra effort of moving against the wind rather than with it—anything to crowd out the ignominious memory.

Without realizing what he was doing, he automatically turned onto Shore Road. It was the shortest distance home. The wind was quite wild here, and the rain beat on his face, but neither the wind nor the rain was cold, just refreshingly cool after two months of heat.

He heard his name called above the din of the rain.

"Mannheim!"

He grimaced and kept walking. He wasn't about to stop and have a shouting match with Bushman in the midst of a heavy downpour.

He heard the call several more times but plodded on without responding. He even giggled internally: Private Mannheim would never have dared to disregard a summons from the stern Nazi officer in another time and place. Let the son of a bitch go jump in the lake.

He was near the entrance to the dock when a hand grabbed his shoulder from the rear and spun him around.

"Don't you walk away from me when I call you!

Your redheaded friend did that, and see what it got him!"

Eric Bushman was dressed in a trench coat, the uniform of a spy, and a hat, which just at that moment was snatched by the wind and sent sailing like a Frisbee down the road. Bushman moved to grab it but was too late. The bullet head was promptly drenched, but the icy blue eyes and the distorted lips continued to flash contempt.

Rudolf Mannheim peered up at the man who towered over him and was not afraid. That was the wonder of it, he did not feel intimidated at all. Perhaps it was an intoxication from his exertions, perhaps he had at long last had enough of Bushman's bullying.

He shrugged out of Bushman's grasp. "Stay away from me, Bushman," he said.

Bushman held his hands up, palms out. "No offense, Rudi," he said, attempting an apologetic smile. "The police are asking questions, and I must know what you intend to tell them. I'm sorry about the rain—"

"I suggest you chase down your hat," Mannheim said. "You're getting soaked."

"The devil with the hat. Just tell me, then I can go after my hat, and you can go home."

"Tell you what? I don't see that it's any business of yours, whatever it is."

Bushman slouched in a mimicry of feebleness. "I'm an old man, Rudi"—the voice was almost a whine—"older than you by fifteen years. All I have left is my reputation, my long and honorable service to our great country—"

Mannheim made a growling noise in his throat.

"Yes! Even you can't deny that. I might even say *distinguished* service. So I was shocked at what you said to me yesterday. Your awful question implied that I had something to do with the unfortunate explosion at Engelhart's. Rudi, Rudi, believe me, I would never do such a thing, I am not able. I bore no animus toward the man, not after all these years. It would be irrational if I did, and I'm a rational man—"

Mannheim studied the face of the man he had hated and feared all his adult life. Rainwater streamed down the face, but he was sure that no tears joined the flow. The old bastard was doing a number on him, as the saying goes, and Mannheim determined to retaliate. No one could blame him if he caused the man to catch pneumonia.

He interrupted the flow of pleading words. "If you want to know what I'm going to say to the police, I'll tell you. Come into my office, and I'll tell you."

He went through the gateway to the dock.

Bushman followed him, exaggerating his limp. "Out on the dock? This is a terrible joke."

"Come on, Lieutenant." Mannheim walked out on the dock, leaning sideways against the slanting wind and rain.

And Bushman followed, protesting. "You've always resented me, Rudi, ever since that time in Italy. You must understand, I was only doing my duty, I had *orders*. Now please tell me, so I can go home and get out of this deluge. I'm an old man, Rudi, an old man."

Mannheim plodded on. At the far end of the dock he looked down at the landing float buffeted by choppy waves. He moved to the southern corner of the dock, halted, and put down the shopping bag. "Mother Nature," he said expansively. "I love to see her manifestations. Don't you find this thrilling, Bushman?"

The icy expression had returned to Bushman's face. "Let's cut out the playacting, Mannheim. Are you going to slander me to the police, or are you going to do the honorable thing and leave me alone in my old age?"

Mannheim peered at him. The man wasn't even winded from the exertion of hobbling the length of the dock. The son of a bitch was in better physical shape than he was. And beneath the cloak of the American flag he was the same shining paragon of the master race that he was in his Nazi uniform.

"I'm going to do the honorable thing, Herr Lieutnant—"

"Please, Rudi, don't keep throwing that old title at me—"

Mannheim raised his voice. "I'm going to do the honorable thing by telling the police that you're a Nazi criminal and that you should be investigated in the death of my friend, Fred Engelhart—"

"Preposterous!"

"That you were commissioned by the Gauleiter of Munich to track down Mr. Engelhart and, what was the expression, 'bring him to justice.' Since Nazi justice no longer exists, that can only mean to exterminate him, hoist him on his own petard, so to speak, to blow him up as he would have blown up your precious master—"

"You're a crazy man! I had nothing to do with— You can't prove—"

"Maybe the police can. All I can do is tell them what I know. That when we talked yesterday you said the fire caught you by surprise—"

"As it did everyone, you dunderhead!"

"You said you didn't expect that a little explosion would start such a massive fire. That was a peculiar thing to say unless you knew the size of the explosive. And just now you implied very strongly that Fred Engelhart was killed because he impolitely turned his back on you. Yes, you did! And that's the sign of a megalomania as large as Hitler's."

Bushman wasn't an "old man" anymore. He drew himself up to his imposing height, uncowed by the wind, unafflicted by the pelting rain. "I see that you're bent on destroying me," he said. "But nothing will come of it—"

"Maybe not, but there'll be an investigation, and maybe we'll find out what happened to the Engelhart family after you failed to catch up to Fred—"

"He was captured by the Americans, everybody knows that."

"So you took your rage out on his family—"

Bushman shook his head. "Now you're really stretching it, Mannheim. The State Department has a full record of my background in Germany—"

"I'm betting that they don't. Even they wouldn't hire

a full-fledged war criminal. I'm betting that there are records in Munich or in the Allied archives or in the files of the Jewish investigators that show what happened to the Engelharts. You see, I have a personal interest—"

Mannheim saw the signs, the sudden rigidity of the face, that showed his rambling indictment had hit a tender spot. He saw the small blue eyes move from him to the wild waters of the bay behind him, then the slight shifting of balance—and he knew that the old Nazi was about to attack.

Bushman sprang with remarkable quickness. His hands were on the smaller man's chest ready for the powerful shove that would catapult him backward into the water. And Mannheim crumpled, clutched the trench coat with both hands and assisted the man's forward thrust over his own falling body. The hands on his chest tried to halt the dive but were unable to grasp the material of the slicker.

Mannheim scrambled to his feet. Like many small men he had never been allowed to feel that he was the equal of larger boys and had sought for an equalizer. Some find it in a handgun or a switchblade. Young Rudi Mannheim had found it in jujitsu, a short-lived fad among youth in Frankfurt. He had gone to no more than a dozen classes before he was called into the *Wehrmacht.* That was forty-five years ago. He had forgotten all about it until the old Nazi attacked him on a dock that projected into Little Neck Bay. He had met the first charge, now he turned to meet the second. But there was no one there. He was alone.

He was only a step from the edge of the dock. He took the step and looked down. Bushman's body was slipping slowly off the landing float into the bay, being shaken off by the tossing motions of the water. He saw the red gash on the head where it had struck the edge of the float. Then the body was in the water, floating away at a remarkable speed, sinking as the heavy material of the trench coat became a lead weight. Then the body was gone.

A thousand thoughts fought for his attention and lost. A fleeting impression that he had somehow duplicated an action by Fred Engelhart. He felt hypnotized by the pitching water.

At length he picked up the shopping bag and trudged away.

He spoke for a few minutes with Eileen Engelhart and that Thatcher kid.

Then he went home.

Prudence believed what he said.

It was she who called the police.

13.

"Everybody's guilty."

It was the Saturday before Columbus Day, six weeks after the Great Savage Point Fire. Ralph Simmons designed the informal get-together not as a celebration of anything but a sort of closing ceremony, an ending to a painful period of tension. As he said to Lillian, "We all gotta let our breath out and stop bellyaching about what happened. I'm mad as hell, and I'm not gonna take it anymore."

Mostly Ralph threw the party for Eileen as a tacit exhortation to her to get off his back. At first he was flattered by her dependence on him to help her in her frenetic search for the killer of her father, even though he realized it was a form of reverse sexism, the young woman wielding the older man as an implement for confronting bureaucracies that considered all young women to be featherbrained. He admitted ruefully that they made a good team, with him playing Tonto to her Lone Ranger or, rather, the lance in the hand of her Lancelot. He truly loved her, but after six weeks of jittery activity he was pooped. Deeply, deeply pooped.

Strangely, when he asked Eileen for the names of young friends to invite, he was surprised that she had so few close friends in the area. And Teddy Thatcher—

who else?—was the only one who could make it. The other attendees were middle-aged or older:

Eddie Epstein and date. Eddie, the lawyer, had been a constant companion in the weeks following Fred Engelhart's death, as he went through the process of gathering the decedent's assets. It was a groping in the dark since all Engelhart's records went up in the fire. The process was still going on, but he could assure Eileen that she was a very wealthy woman. Eddie was happily divorced, and his date was a bouncy butterball in her thirties named Nancy.

Then there were Rudolf and Prudence Mannheim. Mannheim had gone through a period of refusing to show himself outside his house. His first inclination after that terrible day in the rain had been to remain silent about the incident. He had begun to shake as he sat in the kitchen with Prudence, and she had wrapped him in a blanket. When he continued to sit while telling his disjointed story to the homicide detective instead of seeking the higher ground, she knew he was in a state of shock. The only detail of the story that he left out was the assistance he had given to the old man's lunge by way of jujitsu. It was Bushman's lack of agility that brought about his plunge off the dock. Surely no one could suspect a white-bearded little old psychologist of engaging in a martial art.

Despite the eminence of the victim, the admitted existence of ancient enmity, and the blurry details of the fatal encounter on the dock, Lieutenant Joseph Carbine did not detain him as a material witness but, in effect, confined him to quarters while Bushman's background was investigated.

The body was found by divers two days later. The gash on the head strengthened the suspicion of foul play, but the statements of Teddy Thatcher and Eileen Engelhart that when they met Mannheim they could see into his open shopping bag and no bludgeon was hidden there saved Mannheim from arrest.

The personnel file at the State Department was skimpy indeed, citing only Eric Bushman's bare military record and his linguistic talents. But an anonymous functionary at State, who apparently retained a hatred of the Nazis, was able to send to the NYPD copies of records of the infamous People's Court that showed Bushman as the arresting officer in a number of questionable cases, some Jewish, some not. Among the latter was that of the Engelhart family. The only evidence against the family in the record was their relationship with the missing Friedrich, the unrecorded statement of a woman named Kohlkopf, and a year-old White Rose letter discovered in the house by the arresting officer.

The brass at One Police Plaza sent word to the precinct to go easy on the case of the "accidental" death of Eric Bushman, the distinguished foreign service officer. Rudolf Mannheim was thus "cleared" of suspicion.

There were nine people at Ralph's get-together. The ninth was Teddy's mother, Marlene Thatcher. Ralph felt obliged to invite her rather than leave her alone in her big house. He was surprised that Teddy was home from college for the Columbus Day weekend.

The police had been busy, but to Eileen their efforts seemed halfhearted if not downright incompetent. They interviewed everyone and came up with nothing. "They're sleepwalking!" she exclaimed.

The only hard evidence was the fragmentary remains of a detonator culled from the rubble. It could have been a detonator, the police didn't know for sure. Eileen and her assistant bugged Detective Carbine into consulting the famous psychic, Penelope Potter, who happened to live in Savage Point.

More to shut Eileen up than in the expectation of finding anything out, Carbine took a sandwich bag containing the fragments to Penelope's house. It was a gray morning, and the house stood starkly alone in the acres of devastation. With Carbine were Eileen and Ralph and the ever-present Teddy Thatcher, so blond and unintrusive as to be scarcely visible.

They were shown into Penelope's cavernous office, lighted only by a low-wattage lamp on a side table near the conversational grouping of furniture. Little daylight succeeded in poking around the edges of the length of canvas that covered the great window.

Penelope Potter seemed to have shriveled. She crouched rather than sat in her straight-back chair. To Ralph she looked to be about a hundred and five years old. Her husband, Philemon, had always appeared to Ralph to be a nonperson, just barely a presence. But Penelope obviously was sorely grieved by his loss.

Henrietta and Teddy were pale apparitions behind the others who were seated.

After the requisite introductory murmurs, the police detective placed the bag of fragments on the coffee table in front of this suddenly ancient woman.

In respectful tones Carbine mentioned Penelope's assistance to police in the past. "In this case the missing person might be a murderer. These may be the remnants of a detonator used by that person. It isn't much to go on, but anything you can tell us will be more than we have now."

The old woman didn't move. The silence in the gloomy room deepened. No one said anything.

Just when Ralph thought she had gone away and wasn't about to come back, Penelope reached out and placed a hand on the bag. After a minute she withdrew it.

Carbine opened the top of the bag. "Perhaps if you touch the fragments themselves."

Slowly the hand came forward and entered the bag. It remained there for a moment, then returned to the old woman's lap.

"Come on," Eileen said. "Did you see something, Mrs. Potter? Did you see who it was?"

The aged psychic continued to gaze dully at the bag.

"I felt an explosion," she said in a dreamlike voice. "That's all. An explosion."

"Who did it?" Eileen demanded.

The woman shook her head.

Carbine said, "Did you get any sense of the remote control that set it off?"

Penelope Potter continued to shake her head. "I saw a garage, then it disappeared," the thin voice said. "Something interfered, I don't know what it was. Something rippled . . . like silk cloth in a wind . . . and . . . I'm afraid that's all."

They all threw further questions at her, and the woman continued to shake her head apologetically.

When they finally left, the lieutenant returned to the precinct and organized a search of every garage in Savage Point. They found many remote control devices for garage doors, but nothing that would activate a detonator.

A week later Henrietta called Ralph and said that neither she nor her employer, Miss Potter, recalled the name of the detective but that Miss Potter had a message for him. Miss Potter had figured out what the silken thing might be—water. The device might be under water. She didn't know what water. Just water.

Carbine told Ralph, "It's a good out for the old fraud. What she's saying is, the damn thing is at the bottom of the bay. And it just might be, but that's a hell of a big bay full of mud, and there's no way we could find it. Thanks for the information, Simmons."

"Everybody's guilty," Ralph said. He stood by his makeshift bar and scowled at his guests. "I brought you here to change the subject, but you refuse to stop brooding. This is the dullest party I've ever been at. So, okay, let's talk about it and get it over with. Who wants to start?"

Lillian said, "I don't think this is a good idea, Ralph."

"I agree," said Eddie Epstein. "I'll tell you why this is a dull party. It's because the damn host is standing in front of the bar protecting his precious booze from his thirsty guests. I need another drink, damn it." He stood up. "Who's with me?"

Butterball Nancy bounced to her feet. "Me!"

The others looked at him and shrugged.

Prudence Mannheim said, "Well, maybe a little more apple juice." She held up her glass.

Epstein took it, saying, "I hope you're not driving."

"No, we walked," she said uncertainly.

Ralph said, "See what I mean." He refilled several of the glasses. Then he said, "Okay, we're all guilty because our houses didn't burn down."

Marlene Thatcher yawned delicately. "I must be deficient in sensibility," she said. "But I'm not aware of feeling guilty. On the contrary, I'm grateful that it was somebody else and not me."

Eileen Engelhart said, "My house *did* burn down, Uncle Ralph."

"I'm sorry, sweetie," Ralph said. "I guess what I was trying to say is that we've all had twinges of the survivor syndrome. Your father died, and you didn't. Maybe I'm deficient in sensibility too, but hasn't the thought crossed your mind that if you had been there with him, you'd have somehow been able to save him?"

"That's nutty."

"Nutty or not, you thought it, didn't you?"

"Maybe."

Ralph sighed. "I'm only trying to show that all our guilts are nutty. So the hell with them, and let's have some fun! We used to have some fun playing Twenty Questions. You know, where one of us thinks of a person or thing—animal, vegetable, or mineral—and the others try to guess it by asking questions that can be answered by yes or no. Okay, I'm thinking of something. You start, Rudi. Ask me a question."

Mannheim gave him a tight smile. "I'm not very good at games."

Eileen said, "I have a question. Are you the person who killed my father?"

"No." Ralph looked around at apathetic faces.

Mannheim spoke up, to Ralph's surprise. "Ralph, I'd like to hear what these people think . . . since I'm one of the suspects."

"Baloney," Ralph said. "Nobody connects you to Fred's murder. Do you see what I mean when I say everybody's guilty? Let's all concentrate on Rudi's head, he's got a guilt in there—this is known as faith healing—he's got a guilt in there that needs to be evicted. Are we concentrating?"

"He doesn't have much hair," Lillian said.

"No, it's all moved down to his chin. Think of the guilt as a spot, and we all say together, 'Out, damned spot! Out, I say!' Not out loud, just think it ... Now!"

Prudence Mannheim was the first one to laugh, a hearty contralto that triggered laughs from the others.

Even her husband smiled self-consciously. "It's not very professional, Ralph."

"No, but it's scientific," Ralph said. "Christian Scientists do it all the time. Did it work? How do you feel?"

"Like a damn fool."

"Great, great," Ralph said. "Now, to make a short game shorter so we can get on to the serious business of hilarity, let me summarize. Excluding Rudolf Mannheim as a suspect, the only major suspects of the police are dead. Todd Gilchrist died yesterday at the burn unit at Nassau County Medical Center—"

"Did he say anything before he died?" Eileen asked.

"He was in a coma, sweetie. The police got him dead to rights for setting fire to his own house and unintentionally killing the Cat Woman. And he was seen by witnesses walking hastily away from the corner of Schmidt's Lane right after the explosion. Not much of a case, in view of the differences in M.O.'s—"

No one offered comment, so Ralph continued. "The other police suspect, of course, is Eric Bushman, who came a cropper when he tried to dispatch Rudi here to a watery grave. There's no doubt he was a murderous old prick, but there's no clear evidence tying him to Fred's death, only the history of malice that goes back to wartime Munich. But it's a persuasive history—"

"Ralph," Lillian said, "let someone else talk for a while."

He put on a hurt look. "Very well, my love. It's your game, Eileen. You have the floor, and don't talk too long or you-know-who will be after you."

When Eileen smiled, even though tightly, Ralph knew he was succeeding in lightening the mood.

"I'm not sure either one of them is the one," she said. "But if I had to choose between them, I'd pick the murderous old prick, as you say. I have this feeling that the whole thing goes back to Germany."

"I'm afraid you're being romantic, my dear," Marlene Thatcher interposed. "The evil of Nazi Germany reaching forty-five years into the future? It's the stuff of thrillers. Of course, I'm an ignoramus when it comes to history—"

"A very gracious ignoramus," Ralph said.

"You're not supposed to agree with me, Ralph. You're supposed to say, No, no, you're very knowledgeable, dear Marlene. In any event, I'd like to vote in Eileen's game. Does a resident alien have that right?"

"This is a democratic, equal-opportunity household," Ralph said. "Is it all right with you, Eileen?"

"Sure."

Marlene said, "I simply want to vote for that Gilchrist person. I mean, after all, he's a proven murderer, he had a certain animus toward Mr. Engelhart, and he was seen at the scene. *Quod erat demonstrandum.* I rest my case."

Rudolf Mannheim stood up. "No, Mrs. Thatcher."

Good, good, thought Ralph, he's coming out of his funk.

Mannheim said, "Your Mr. Gilchrist was a bumbler—"

"*My* Mr. Gilchrist?"

Mannheim didn't seem to hear her. "If Gilchrist wanted to blow up Fred's house, he'd have blown himself up as well, just as he wound up killing himself when he set fire to his own house. No, I'm convinced that the one who did this was Eric Bushman. I knew the man and—"

"We *all* knew him, for goodness sake," Marlene interrupted.

"Not the vicious man underneath," Mannheim said. "He was commissioned to find and kill Fred Engelhart, and he did."

DEATHSTORM 135

"We have only your word for that, Mr. Mannheim." Marlene Thatcher's tone was still civil, but the attitude was imperious.

"Not entirely," Mannheim said. "The records show that he was attached to the Gauleiter's staff, and he was the arresting officer in the case of Fred's family in Munich—"

"If true, that was forty-five years ago. And Bushman had become a doddering old man who was incapable of killing anyone!"

"I grant you that it's possible he hired someone to do the actual bombing, but—"

"Who? I'm sure in your imagination you must know whom he hired to do the job! It would be someone with access to explosives, wouldn't it? There are a number of contractors who live in this community, I've been introduced to several—"

Ralph said, "I think we're getting a little heated, folks."

Mannheim looked at him and let his shoulders slump. "We did get carried away, didn't we? All I'm saying is that Eric Bushman was a diehard Nazi, and he was probably the one who killed Fred Engelhart."

"Nazi schmotzy," Marlene said in a humorous tone. "I don't believe for a minute that even a diehard Nazi would go after the Engelhart family without cause. God knows I hold no brief for the Nazis, but they weren't *all* insane. If he arrested the family, he must have been given solid evidence by that informant, what was the name? No, I vote for the suspect nearer to home, that Gilchrist person. You said I could vote, didn't you?"

Ralph said, "You have heard the evidence, ladies and gentlemen of the jury—"

Lillian said, "Hey, I thought we were detectives."

He went through the charade of taking a vote, which took five minutes, then intoned the results: Todd Gilchrist—two; Eric Bushman—two; None of the above—two; Both of the above—two. And one voted for the butler. "The bar is now reopened," he announced.

Ralph had succeeded in getting them to let their breath out and relax . . . somewhat.

Later Marlene Thatcher joshed Rudolf Mannheim. "You just didn't have a case, counselor, or should I say solicitor?"

Mannheim made a face. "You're right, Mrs. Thatcher. But I'm so involved in this that I'm going to Munich in the spring and do a little digging. I haven't been back to Germany since the war, and I think it's about time I made a visit to the land of my birth. Prudence has been after me to go. She's part Dutch, and that's close to Deutsch—"

Eddie Epstein said, "The only solicitor I ever knew hung out at Eighth Avenue and Forty-second Street—"

Bouncing Nancy said, "Aha! A confession!"

Lillian said, "I don't get it."

Everyone was talking and laughing. Ralph made some jokes about street-corner lawyers, and the subject of Fred Engelhart's death was forgotten.

Later when Ralph and Lillian were alone in the kitchen cleaning up, he said, "Did dear Lady Marlene's demeanor strike you as peculiar?"

"Well, she sure jumped down Rudi's throat, if that's what you mean."

"Yes, that," Ralph said. "And she seemed to know more about Eric Bushman's history than I thought. Carbine told me about the arrest of Fred's family back in Munich, but I never told anyone else, not even Eileen—I figured she was disturbed enough as it was. Oh, well, I suppose Carbine told other people besides me."

"You know who I miss?" Lillian said. "Angel Jones. She was really a very nice person. She had a good sense of humor."

"Hey," Ralph said. "I just thought of something. We've been thinking someone was out to kill Fred. Suppose, just suppose the murderer was really after Angel and not Fred. We really don't know anything about her, she was just there—"

"Ralph—"

"She was really very peculiar—"
"Ralph—"
He stopped talking.
"Let's go to bed, Ralph."
"Good idea."
They went to bed.

14.

The rebuilding of Savage Point proceeded slowly. Judith the architect, making use of the old foundation and a speedy insurance settlement, was the first to raise a skeletal framework and a roof before the winter halt. To Ralph it looked like an ordinary framework for an ordinary house until Judith showed him her rendition of the finished structure: the siding of the entire house was going to be mirrored glass, like many of the skyscrapers in the city or, perhaps, the sunglasses on a state trooper. It struck him as being both idiotic and sinister, but he said, "It's one of a kind, Judy, one of a kind!" And she was pleased.

The only others who moved as quickly as Judith were the vultures. Many of the older residents whose homes were destroyed decided not to rebuild, as did the estates of the handful who died. So they sold the lots to the contractors, speculators, and agents who swarmed around them. A basic building lot, sixty by a hundred, brought two hundred thousand dollars, double lots brought four hundred thousand. But winter came quickly, and the swath of the fire remained pretty much a doleful no-man's land through the winter months.

Penelope Potter, in the wake of the fire and the death of her husband, was shaken out of her religious depression by a refreshing cascade of money. Many years ago she had gotten her real-estate agent's license along with her sainted husband.

When several of her burned-out neighbors came to her with their lots for sale, she put up a sign in front of her house: "Penelope Potter—Let Me Help You with Your Real Estate Problems." Her secretary did most of the work, while Penelope played the mystic beneath her new stained-glass window depicting St. Joseph, the Rail-Splitter. The two of them brokered dozens of sales for tidy six percent commissions.

Bill Greaney, the undertaker, earned enough to buy a winter retreat on Florida's Gulf Coast.

Eileen Engelhart remained with the Simmonses for another month after the Columbus Day weekend; then, in a spurt of decision making, she bought a condo near Washington Square and she dumped Teddy Thatcher. Ralph and Lillian heard fragments of the final scene from their bedroom.

Eileen and Teddy were downstairs on the sofa, talking softly. The television was on with the sound turned low out of consideration for the old folks upstairs. Ralph and Lillian were lying in bed waiting for sleep to come.

Suddenly Eileen's voice was raised. Teddy must have used the expression, "You know me," because Eileen said, "No, I *don't* know you! Not who you really are . . . Hello, is anyone in there?"

Ralph imagined her rapping on Teddy's forehead or peeking up his nose or some such action to dramatize her words.

Eileen's voice: "No, no, I mean it. I don't know how you feel about *anything*. Not even the weather. I hear it rains a lot in England. Do you like the rain? You never say . . . So, okay, you like the sunshine. Hey, now we're getting somewhere . . . Answer me one question. Why did you drop out of Virginia? . . . I know, you told me that. Pardon me, Teddy, but I don't believe it. You didn't stay here just to help me. I think you stayed because of your mother . . . Oh, shit, no, I'm *not* calling you a momma's boy. Look, I appreciate your helping me, I really do . . ."

The voices lowered to murmurs, and Lillian muttered, "Goody, I think she's giving him the boot."

Eileen's voice rose again. "If you insist, one of the reasons I'm moving into the city is to get away from you. That's not the only reason. I've got to get on with my life, damn it . . . Aw, come on, lover, don't be like that, it's not the end of the world . . . No, no, you're good in bed, I'll give you a letter of recommendation . . . I didn't mean to joke, sorry about that."

Ralph said to Lillian, "Would you give me a letter of recommendation?"

Thirty seconds later he said, "Would you?"

"I'm thinking about it," she said.

"Ouch."

She said, "No, I wouldn't."

"Well, at least you thought about it. That's something."

The next morning at breakfast Eileen announced somberly, "I broke off with Teddy last night. He scared me. He said I couldn't do that to him."

"What did you say?"

"I said, 'Watch me.' I didn't handle it right, Uncle Ralph. But it came over me all of a sudden that he gave me the creeps."

"Don't worry about it," Ralph said. "With you in the Village, he'll be out of your life."

"He said he was going to enroll at NYU to be near me."

"You think he might try something?"

"God, who knows? Sometimes it seems like his mind's a blank, and he never gets excited about anything—except last night. He acted like I insulted him."

Lillian put a hand on Eileen's arm. "Forget about him. You'll find yourself a nice starving artist, and you'll live it up on jugs of wine and feel superior to people who're earning a living and having children. Then you'll get in with the espresso crowd who speak in tongues. Then you'll meet a nice divorced man in your condo building. If you're lucky he'll be tall and strong so he can keep creeps from bothering you, like maybe engineering students from NYU. And at least once a month you'll come back here and learn how smart your Uncle Ralph and Aunt Lillian really are, even if they don't understand how anything can be postmodern—I mean, modern is modern—or how deconstructionists can communicate anything worthwhile listening to, or how anyone can consider Andy Warhol a serious artist, or—"

Ralph said, "So much for the Philistine's view of Bohemia. Lil once had an apartment in Chelsea, and that made her an expert on Greenwich Village. But she's right. You're in for some exciting times down there. Are you going back to school?"

Eileen grinned. "I thought I'd study art, but after listening to Aunt Lillian, maybe I ought to settle down with the English creep."

The next day she packed her few things into her cuddly new electric-red Alfa Romeo and departed for a new life in Sin City.

Ralph and Lillian settled in old routines. Not a day went by that they didn't think of Fred Engelhart and the good times they had had in the bell tower. And once a month they visited his grave in St. John's Cemetery off Woodhaven Boulevard. They knew Fred had been raised a Catholic, hence the choice of a Catholic cemetery. But it took some lying to get Angel Jones in the neighboring plot. She was his wife, they told the authorities, and the assumption was that she had converted. Who could say that she didn't? And so Fred and Angel rested side by side in hallowed ground. Ralph hoped that that was okay with Fred.

And the fall months slid into winter. Ralph called Lieutenant Joseph Carbine several times and was told that the case was still open but that the investigation had come to a dead end.

The trouble was, nobody was sure it was murder.

The first real snowstorm came on New Year's Eve, about eight inches of it. The city was prepared, the major arteries were plowed and salted, but backwater areas, like Savage Point, were the last to get attention.

Ralph and Lillian had planned another good-riddance gathering long before the snow appeared on the computer's grid. Eileen Engelhart phoned at the last minute to ask how the streets were, and when Ralph told her they were barely passable they agreed she should stay at her new home in Manhattan and not take a chance of getting stranded in the boondocks. So the party consisted of the same old eight faces, minus Eileen.

In accordance with the theme of the party, Ralph placed a large trash can by the front door, and the guests, as they arrived, tossed into it something they were happy to be rid of. Lillian threw in eight diet books, one at a time, and an old girdle. "I've given up trying," she said. "I was born of peasant stock, and God intended me to be a tiller of the soil. I wasn't meant to be an aristocratic thoroughbred like Marlene, who can eat anything she wants and never put on an ounce. I hate you, Marlene. So good riddance to bad rubbish!"

Ralph threw in his handyman book. "God intended me to be a hirer of repairmen," he said. "But He didn't give me the money to pay them."

Prudence Mannheim showed a rare sense of humor by throwing in her husband's concertina. "All he knows how to play is that German war song, 'Lilli Marlene,'" she said. "And he mangles that poor lady like Jack the Ripper. So R.I.P. to the Ripper."

Rudolf Mannheim placed a large paper bag in the trash can.

"What's in the bag, Rudi?"

"Nothing."

"Come on, tell us."

"Well . . . Just some things I wanted to get rid of. A garage door opener that doesn't work. A pair of old boots, my army boots as a matter of fact, and a wool scarf that Prudence's cousin knitted for me years ago—"

"You didn't!" Prudence exclaimed.

"The dear woman didn't know where to stop," Mannheim explained. "It's so long I can wrap it around me three times and I still trip over the ends."

Ralph dumped a stack of old newspapers. "Stories of what happened," he said.

Marlene Thatcher said, "Oh, dear, I didn't think you meant it, Ralph. So I didn't bring anything. It's been a horrid year in some respects, but it was also the year I got to know my good neighbors, and I don't want to throw that away. Oh, dear . . ." She turned to her son. "Teddy, did you bring something?"

The young man shrugged. "I really should throw away my blasted car, but it won't quite fit in there. Besides, it's at the repair shop, so I'm driving what they call a *loaner*. There's a pun for you, Uncle Ralph. It's all yours."

"I don't accept gift puns," Ralph said with dignity.

Eddie Epstein lifted his lady friend, Butterball Nancy, and placed her in the can. "Farewell," he wailed. "It was nice while it lasted, but all good things must come to an end."

Nancy's whole body was jiggling with her giggles, to Ralph's great delight.

"Yes, the good times are over, ladies and gentlemen," Epstein announced. "I'm going to marry the wench!"

Everyone was exclaiming at once, and the party got off to a happy start, as all New Year's Eve parties should. Only Teddy Thatcher was glum.

Ralph said to him, "I got some port wine specially for you, kid. It's the perfect drink for a cold and snowy night."

"Thanks," Teddy said listlessly.

"And it's great for putting out old flames," Ralph said. "You and Eileen are too young to be getting serious."

Teddy said sullenly, "Romeo and Juliet were only fourteen."

"And see what happened to them," Ralph said.

Since none of them were habitual drinkers of alcohol

and all were within walking distance of their homes, inhibitions soon wound up in the trash can too, and jollity reigned. Ralph played his old Benny Goodman records, and he and Lillian put on a version of jitterbugging as performed by arthritic oldsters.

Then Ralph retrieved the concertina from the trash can—Prudence hadn't seriously meant to discard it—and handed it to Mannheim, saying, "Play, Fiddle, Play."

"I don't know any new music," Mannheim said. "Just a few polkas."

"Who cares? Play."

Ralph watched Marlene dancing with great abandon to the old continental music, and he marveled at how her ladyship, who had originally come on as an aristocratic snob, was now showing such earthy high spirits. Partly it was the glow of alcohol, he figured, but it seemed to be the music itself that enlivened her. She slipped into a cancan, and Epstein cried, "Ooh-la-la!" Then inevitably Rudolf Mannheim played "Lilli Marlene" and started to sing the words in German.

Marlene Thatcher said, "No, no, in English."

"I don't know the English," he said.

"Like this, you *dumkopf*," she said and started singing along with him in English: "Underneath the lantern by the barrack gate—Darling, I remember the way you used to wait . . ."

It was a thin voice but with a sort of—Ralph searched for the proper words—sincere belief in the truth of the sentimental words that good popular singers have. They all applauded when she finished, and she suddenly became self-conscious and retreated to her chair.

Ralph said, "You know who you remind me of? That other Marlene—Marlene Dietrich."

"You flatter me, Ralph," she said. "But you have the wrong country. That Marlene was German, no?"

"Matter of fact, you're better looking than her," he said. "And you have sexier legs. Could we see the legs again?"

Lillian said, "Ease up, Ralph, you're tripping over your tongue."

At midnight Mannheim did a bad rendition of "Auld Lang Syne," and everybody kissed. Butterball Nancy, apparently feeling sorry for the tall, handsome, and stiff Teddy Thatcher, had been playing up to him for the last hour and, at the kissing hour, locked him in an embrace that had him squirming.

In the lull of exhaustion that set in a half hour later, Ralph sat next to Rudi Mannheim and asked if he still planned a trip to Germany in the spring. Mannheim said he already had the tickets. He said he was indeed going to make inquiries in Munich. "For my own peace of mind," he said.

Ralph lowered his voice. "It struck me tonight that it might be interesting to track down that woman who made the complaint against Fred's family, see if there was a connection to Eric Bushman. I wouldn't waste too much time on it, but—the name was Kohlkopf. She's probably long since dead, and whatever records there were are probably in some Allied archives somewhere. So, as I say—"

He was interrupted by Marlene Thatcher announcing that she had had a glorious time and it was time to mush on home. "Come, Teddy," she said, and the quiet young man came from somewhere behind Ralph and followed her to the entry hall, muttering thanks for a good time.

A short time later Eddie Epstein and his Nancy left. His last comment to Ralph was, "That Thatcher dame is hot as a pistol. Any time you have 'Legs' Thatcher over, I'll be happy to join you."

Mannheim seemed reluctant to leave. He wanted to stay and chat, but his eyes would close and he would stop in midsentence. Ralph offered coffee. He offered a choice of spare rooms to spend the night in. Prudence pulled him to his feet, however, got him into his greatcoat and boots, and they finally left.

Cleaning up in the kitchen, Ralph and Lillian agreed it had been a good party. They discussed Eddie Epstein's new fiancèe. Lillian said, "I should have given those darn diet books to her." Ralph said, "Maybe it's just her peasant stock." Lillian punched him in the arm. Their verdict was that she was a good match for Eddie. Ralph said, "I bet she's dynamite in bed," and Lillian punched him again. They abandoned the cleaning-up chores and went to bed themselves.

Dover Street had not yet been plowed, but there were ruts in the snow where several vehicles, undoubtedly with four-wheel drive, had traversed it. The still falling snow swirled every which way around Rudolf and Prudence Mannheim like a cloud of lacy gnats. They plodded single file in one of the ruts to the corner. Sidewalks would not be shoveled until morning and were quite impassable. Savage Point Road had been plowed an hour or so earlier, however, so they could walk side by side in the middle of the road as they headed toward home.

A great sense of serenity descended on them. There was no noise whatsoever, not even the sound of wind in the wires overhead, just the crunch-crunch of their footsteps. They were walking through the Valley of Peace, the devastation on each side of the road unseen under the covering of snow. Prudence hummed an old song, "Walking in a Winter Wonderland."

"I almost fell asleep in there," Mannheim said in a hushed voice. "But this—this is *heaven*."

"I doubt if it snows in heaven, Rudi," she murmured.

"Eskimo heaven," he said.

They walked on in contentment. They were alone in the universe. No other creature was stirring, not even a mouse. "Wunderbar," he said.

She said, "What were you and Ralph talking about?"

"Oh," he said. "He seems to have a suspicion—"

The sound of a car came to them from the rear.

He said, "How dare they invade our Eskimo heaven!"

They turned, saw the advancing headlights. They moved to the side of the road, faced the oncoming vehicle with smiles on their faces.

The vehicle increased speed. It was coming directly at them. They waved in alarm and backed into the deep snow. He yelled, "Hey!"

The vehicle smashed into them point-blank and continued over their bodies. Rudolf's last thought was to shield her body with his. Then the snow-white universe turned to eternal darkness.

15.

The snowfall of New Year's Eve was the only normal meteorological event of that winter. Spring came in January. Flowers that had survived the desert conditions of summer and had gone into restorative hibernation woke up and arched their petals, undone by their interior imperatives. New York City was in a water crisis, but the people shrugged. Who cared, so long as the temperature lingered in the fifties. Meteorologists spoke of the depletion of the ozone layer caused by spray deodorants and other products of civilization. So what?

Ralph Simmons developed a low-grade pain in his stomach, which wouldn't go away. His doctor indulged him by having him undergo a GI series at North Shore Hospital. Ralph made jokes about the humiliating procedure, but no physical cause of the pain was found. "It's all in your head, Ralph," Boomer Smith said. Ralph called him a quack.

"So how come you're drumming your fingers on my desk?" Boomer shouted.

It was then that Ralph realized that the death of Rudolf Mannheim had put him in a state of anxiety. By the time a lonely plowman had discovered the bodies of the Mannheims two hours after they had been hit, the continuing snowfall had obliterated the marks of the vehicle that had run them down. In fact, if the man hadn't been trying to widen the passable roadbed, the bodies might have gone undetected for a much longer time, possibly until a neighborhood dog unearthed them in the morning. By that time Prudence Mannheim would have been dead as well. Rudolf's body was on top of hers, and she would have been smothered or frozen to death.

She was taken to Booth Memorial Hospital in Flushing, where she remained in a coma for many days. Her physical injuries did not account for it. Fractured ribs and the left tibia were easily treated. She had a severe concussion but no fractured skull. The coma was caused by the drastic reduction of oxygen reaching her brain, doctors figured. When she finally came out of the coma, she didn't remember a thing about the accident —or anything else. The doctors were unable to predict whether she would ever regain full use of her brain.

It was obviously a hit-and-run case, and police labeled it a vehicular homicide. But without evidence of skid marks at the scene or traces of paint or chrome on the clothing of the victims, they were unable to reconstruct the event or impute intent on the part of the driver. On the assumption, in view of the stormy conditions, that the vehicle was a local one, Homicide Lieutenant Joseph Carbine had uniformed cops scanning the front ends of all vehicles in the area. Nothing. He wasn't even sure if the perpetrator was a drunk driver or an intentional killer.

But Ralph Simmons was. Three people—three Germans—were dead. All three were connected to an incident that had occurred in Munich, Germany, over forty-five years ago, symbolized somehow by the White Rose. Ralph could not bring himself to believe it was coincidence. He sensed that the sequence wasn't over. And the pain developed in his stomach.

He told Carbine of this sense of foreboding.

Carbine said, "I'm not happy about it either, Simmons, but we've done all we can. Do you really feel that you're next in line for an accident?"

"It sounds dumb, doesn't it?" Ralph said. "But I've got this gut feeling—"

Carbine said, "Gut feelings are murder in my line of work. I always find that Pepto-Bismol helps." He said it with a tight smile.

During January's heat wave the denizens of Manhattan shmoozed in the daytime but were the victims of a record number of muggings at night. In Savage Point tennis players happily played tennis at the club until strained muscles and tendons halted them; joggers worked up a record amount of sweat; and young mothers perambulated along Shore Road as if it were springtime. Next door to the Simmonses Teddy Thatcher took the tarp off his swimming pool and practiced his crawl, backstroke, and butterfly in the hours that he wasn't attending classes at NYU. It was only when Ralph saw the steam coming off the pool in the night hours that he realized the pool was heated.

Ralph grumbled to Lillian, "With that kind of dough, why did these people choose to settle in little old middle-class Savage Point?"

Teddy hadn't yet tried to invade Eileen's Greenwich Village condo, probably because her building was well guarded by husky private policemen.

Eileen spent a week in Palm Beach as a guest of some new friends and came back to report: "Palm Beach is the pits. There are two kinds of rich people—those who talk and are boring, bore*ring*, and those who talk and I don't understand what they're saying. The only good thing was Disney World."

Ralph asked her what she planned to do with her father's waterfront property. "The foundations are still good," he said. "You have to realize, now that the rubble is cleared away, that the main foundation that Fred made exceptionally deep is a danger to anybody who strays onto the property. At least you should do something about that."

Eileen said, "I don't know. I don't think I could live there. Maybe I ought to sell it. What do you think my father would want?"

"I'm sure he never gave it a thought," Ralph said.

Eileen went with them on their January visit to the cemetery.

The mild weather continued into February. Ralph succeeded in walking off the tension in his stomach. During the reign of the pain he had lost ten pounds. Lillian said, "Keep it off, Ralph, you look like Rambo." Ralph said, "Yo," and she said, "I take it back, you look like Don Knotts."

The second week in February, Lillian decided it was a good time to visit her daughter in Westchester. "If I don't, those children will be strangers," she said. "My own grandchildren!" That Sunday Ralph carried all the toys she had bought for the kids into the city and put her on the train at Grand Central Station. He said, "Let me know when you've had enough." She punched him in the arm. She planned to stay a week and hoped to induce her daughter to drive her back down at the end of that time.

The first day he was alone in the house he felt strangely liberated. "I can do anything I want, and there's no one I have to account to!" He drove to the golf driving range. Lillian never wanted to go with him, so he seldom went. The range was closed. He went to a Taco Bell and splotched the front of his shirt with refried beans. He went on his walking beat. Back home, he turned on television, which he never did in the daytime. He started drinking at five o'clock. At six he called Lillian in Westchester, and she said, "You've had enough, Ralph." That made him angry, so he made himself another martini. He heated a frozen dinner in the microwave and found that it was inedible. He put it outside for Hunter the cat to eat, but the cat hissed and glared at him reproachfully.

The next day he felt lonely.

Eileen called and said, "What are you guys doing for Valentine's Day?"

Ralph said, "That's Sunday. Lillian should be back by then. Come on out, sweetie, and I'll bake you a cherry pie. We'd be delighted to have you."

On Tuesday his walk took him into the fire-devastated zone, which he had been avoiding for the most part because of the memories it dredged up. Some of the builders had taken advantage of January's weather to raise new skeletons over the old. They should have been signs of new life to him, but they weren't. They were reminders that his world was disappearing piece by piece and being replaced by the artifacts of a new generation, making him the alien in what used to be his home ground.

Someone called his name. Pale Henrietta stood on the front step of the Potter house under the incongruous real-estate sign.

"Miss Potter would like a word with you," she said, and led him into St. Joseph's office at the front of the house rather than Penelope's cavernous den in the rear.

Penelope Potter stood up behind St. Joseph's old desk and waved Ralph to a chair. In contrast to the crumpled old woman he had last seen, she now moved with the spryness of a squirrel and peered at him with glittering eyes. It was the perfect spot for a real-estate office; nearly all of the plots she had for sale could be pointed to from the front window.

She went through the ritual of pleasantries like a bored priest at the early-morning mass. Then she peered out the window. "Jesus said, 'I must be about my father's business,' and I must be about my husband's. What does Miss Engelhart plan to do with her father's building site? It's a choice location, but you must realize that the bottom has fallen out of the housing business in the last year, so don't get her hopes up too high. And how are you and that dear wife of yours?"

Ralph had difficulty following her from the temple in Jerusalem to the real-estate business in Savage Point to a concern for the well-being of his dear wife. He stammered replies, then commented on how well she looked. "You were smart to keep busy," he said.

She said, "It has kept me away from my contemplations. Still, we manage to get to church every morning, don't we, Henrietta? The messages I get are short-circuited by the currents of commerce. All the same, I wish to warn you. The white cloud I see over Savage Point is concentrated over Dover Street. Although it is white, I sense that it is evil. That's all I can say . . . Now I must get on with my business."

"Are you predicting snow?" Ralph asked.

"No, no," she said irritably. "Just that something from the past is catching up. Please speak to Miss Engelhart for me, will you?"

Ralph found himself being guided to the front door and out. He pondered her message: *danger lurks*. It reminded him of a ditty from his childhood:

Look out, look out, there's danger everywhere,
Look out, look out, you'd better all take care;
It's better safe than sorry, so you'd better all beware—
Remember, the watchword is caution.

He was surprised that he remembered the tune, and he sang it to himself. He returned from the walk rapt in an aura of nostalgia. This must be the first stage of senility, he thought.

The blizzard slammed into New York on Sunday, St. Valentine's Day.

III. Snowstorm

16.

The meteorologists predicted snow, and the city was prepared to deal with up to a foot of it. What they weren't prepared for was two feet of snow and the whistling winds that made the storm a blizzard.

It started quite tamely early that Sunday morning. Ralph snuggled up in the living room with ten pounds of Sunday *Times* and the happy refrain, "Let it snow, let it snow, let it snow." He wasn't going anywhere. The cherry pie he had baked the previous day was on the kitchen table under plastic wrap. He had carved a heart in the upper crust as a valentine to Eileen. The juice had bubbled up through the cut, making the heart appropriately red. The ingredients had come premixed from the supermarket; he was sure it would win no prizes, but, what the heck, it was the thought that counted.

When Eileen called at noon, there were four to five inches on the ground, and the wind was snarling. She said she was leaving and would be there in an hour.

He said, "They're talking about a lot of snow."

She said, "I want to be with you and Aunt Lillian. You're my only family."

"Maybe we should make it tomorrow or the next day."

"Oh, pooh, I'm coming out, Uncle Ralph. See you."

Ralph felt a sentimental glow even as he commiserated with her obvious loneliness. Why it manifested itself on Valentine's Day and not New Year's Eve, he didn't know.

Lillian called a short time later from Westchester. Her daughter was refusing to drive in the snow. "I've had enough," she said forlornly.

He said, "Try to stick it out another day, honey. I really don't think it would be smart for me to drive up there and then try to get back down."

"I know," she said.

"Go sleigh-riding with the grandchildren. That oughta be fun."

"You're kidding."

A few minutes later he hung up, feeling guilty. He was lonely. Lillian was lonely. Eileen was lonely. Everybody was lonely. The least he could do was clear the path for Eileen when she arrived.

He bundled up, got the snow blower from the basement, dragged it out into the snow, and tried to start it. All it did was cough. The wind blew his hat off, and he had to lumber after it. He got snow in his boots. They were short boots, inadequate for stepping into drifts. He finally got the blower going and found that no matter which direction he aimed the blown snow it lashed back into his face. Thoroughly miserable, he gave up the battle and retreated indoors.

He looked at his watch. Eileen was late. He was hungry but decided to wait for her before eating anything. He settled for a beer.

Traffic on the Long Island Expressway was light, and most of the drivers drove slowly and carefully. Visibility was about thirty feet, and though only about five inches had fallen the wind formed deeper drifts, effectively closing down a lane or two. Enough Sunday drivers and speeders were out, however, to add to the hazards of driving and to form roadblocks where they whammed into abutments and guard rails.

Eileen tooled along alertly in her lovely little Alfa. She shouldn't have come, she knew, but she had just broken up with the rich weirdo who had taken her to Palm Beach, and she felt dislocated. He had some strange ideas about society and about sex. Boy, she sure was great at picking boyfriends! She wondered what Ralph Simmons was like when he was in his twenties. There was something the matter with her, she decided. She seemed unable to form attachments with people her own age, only with parental types like her father and Uncle Ralph and Aunt Lillian.

She swerved around a stalled car and felt her own car start to fishtail. The car straightened out. "Good old Alfie," she said.

Take Teddy Thatcher. Good looking, good manners, English accent. When she went out with him, she felt that other girls had to be jealous of her. God, how superficial can you get! It had taken her a long time to realize he was a creep. The way he was brought up, she supposed. She had the impression that when he was making love he felt he was doing a shameful thing. Nothing she could put her finger on, just the way he seemed strangely modest about his body and the way he tried to suppress his excitement. His way of keeping his cool maybe. Perhaps it had something to do with his mother. In a way she felt sorry for him. He never seemed very happy.

He called her on the phone several times since she moved to the Village—purposeless conversations with long gaps in which she could hear only his breathing, forcing her to invent excuses to hang up. Having used up the obvious ones, like someone's at the door and something's burning on the stove, she recently said, "Did you hear that? There's an accident right outside my window!" And he had said, "No, there isn't, love, the street is clear." The realization that he was within sight of her building, perhaps looking up at her window, gave her an icy chill.

A lightweight panel truck passed her on the left, going too fast. The wind was heaving from the left.

Ahead was an overpass where the wind lost its direction and swirled about in a frenzy. The panel truck was about forty feet ahead of her, barely visible. On the far side of the overpass the again unimpeded wind slammed into the side of the vehicle, pushing it into the lane ahead of her in the process of tipping it over on its side. The brake lights flashed red, and the Alfa was on a collision course.

Eileen woke tardily from her unpleasant reverie, but her young reflexes were good. If she braked she knew she would skid right into the overturning vehicle. If she swerved either left or right she would probably lose control. Without really thinking about it, she held her course for another second. Luckily the momentum of the truck moved it not only sideways but forward, giving her the extra inches she needed. When she felt the renewed force of the wind hit her Alfa, she turned as minimally as she could into the wind toward the left lane being vacated by the truck. At the last fraction of a second she saw that the right rear of her car was going to sideswipe the truck. She turned more sharply into the wind and accelerated, grimacing in expectation of the jolt and the screech of ripping metal.

She was spinning through the snowfall, seeing nothing but the whiteness of the snow, which seemed to be flying horizontally to her right—twirling around her instead of her revolving in it.

She clung to the useless steering wheel in dreadful anticipation. Then she remembered to take her foot off the gas pedal and straighten out the wheels. She thought of her father being propelled through the air by the explosion—it was an image she had constructed in her mind from the location of his body under the tree—and herself spinning madly down the slick surface of the expressway, and said, "This is nutty, it's not the same at all."

Eventually the revolutions slowed, and the car came to a stop, its nose in a deep drift. She slumped in her seat, her thoughts still twirling. Someday she was going to remember this and laugh. Someone up there was playing with her. God was wind, snow, fire ... and death. She shook her head.

Miraculously the car was still on the roadbed, and the motor was purring—rather smugly, she thought. "Hope you enjoyed yourself," she said to the car. "I didn't."

She saw that she was near the Savage Point Road exit. She looked back up the highway, couldn't see anything through the snow. "Damn!" she said to herself. She backed the Alfa out of the drift, turned, and slowly drove back the wrong way to where the panel truck must be, her bright lights on, fearful of being smashed into by another vehicle.

She was almost on it before she saw it. A young man stood beside it in the snow, dressed only in a light jacket. He appeared to be dazed.

She got out, staggered to him, talked to him, forced him to get into her car. "You'd freeze to death," she told him.

All he said was, "The fucking wind."

She drove him beyond her exit to the Little Neck exit, and deposited him in front of the small Deepdale Hospital. "They'll take care of you," she said.

A half hour and several hair-raising moments later she plowed into the deep snow in front of the Simmons house.

"What am I doing here?" she wondered.

Ralph and Eileen had cherry pie and ice cream for lunch, laughing like naughty children. She made fun of the pie because Ralph had had to adapt a second bottom crust to fill the role of upper crust, with the result that it was crummy at the edges. He told her they were "decorative touches."

Her valentine to him was a clay sculpture of two roly-poly figures kissing blissfully. "I don't know," Ralph said. "Couldn't you take a little off her hips. Lil would love it if you did." She trimmed the figure with a kitchen knife. "Now me," Ralph said. She handed him the knife and said, "It goes against my artistic integrity. You do it."

They ran out of things to talk about in midafternoon.

She asked him what he had been like as a young man.

He said, "Thinner."

"No, really."

"I was in the army when I was eighteen," he said. "What was any soldier like? An alien on a faraway planet. When I met my first drill sergeant, I realized it was the planet of the apes. What can I say? I just followed orders. If there weren't orders to follow, I would have been completely lost."

"Sounds like Teddy Thatcher."

"Why do you say that?"

"I don't know. You say you were just following orders. My father was doing the same thing."

"Not when he tried to blow up the good Gauleiter and wound up with Eric Bushman on his tail for the rest of his life."

"Do you think Bushman killed my father?"

"No."

"Who then?"

"The same person who killed Rudi Mannheim. That was long after Bushman himself went to his reward. So he couldn't be your father's murderer."

"Who does that leave?"

"Either a stranger . . . or Teddy Thatcher."

"That's nutty," she said.

He went to the window and peered out at the wild snowscape. "Can't tell if the sun is over the yardarm or not," he said. "I feel like a drink. How about you?"

"Why Teddy?"

"Drink first," he said, and went into the kitchen to get ice.

She followed him. "But Teddy couldn't have. He was on the boat with us. Remember?"

"I remember," he said, dumping ice cubes into a bucket. "I've thought about it often since our New Year's Eve party."

Like a priest at the altar, he reverently created a pitcher of martinis. "James Bond was wrong," he said.

"Stirred, not shaken. When you shake, you drown it in ice water—"

"I think you're losing your mind, Uncle Ralph."

"Bear with me, my daughter," he said in priestly tones. He finished his ritual and handed her drink to her as if it were a holy chalice.

She made a face, took a sip, and said, "Yuk."

"Give it a chance."

She said, "Why Teddy?"

Sitting in his chair, he took a sip and sighed contentedly.

"Now that the vocal cords are properly lubricated, I can speak. Yes, Teddy was on the boat with us. But explosives are quite sophisticated these days. I think the one that killed your father and Angel was set off by remote control. I may be all wet, but I think the gadget that set it off was in the pocket of Teddy's jacket."

"Oh, come on, Uncle Ralph!"

"You'll remember that he kept the jacket on the whole time we were on the boat. A strange garment for a young man of today to be wearing on a summer cruise. But he's a strange young man, isn't he?" He took another sip of martini. "You two were in the front of the boat where I couldn't see you. What did he do?"

"Well, he had the tie-rope in his hands. He was going to tie the boat to the mooring."

"Both hands?"

She frowned. "Not just then. We were sort of rolling toward the buoy. He had the rope in one hand. Then when—"

"Where was his other hand?"

"It was—it was in his pocket, but—"

"I won't push the point any further," Ralph said. "It's the only theory that makes sense. The device was in that pocket."

"Far out," she said.

Suddenly the phone rang. He was surprised when he heard Marlene's civilized voice greeting him with some warmth.

"Isn't this storm something?" she said.

"Sure is a humdinger," he said. "Right out of Lower Slobovia."

"Listen, I noticed your lights on. Has Lillian come back from her daughter's?"

"No, she's snowed-in up there just as we are here."

Marlene said, "They're predicting a lot more snow. Teddy and I are trapped here, bored with our own company, and there you are only fifty feet away, all alone on Valentine's Day. Nobody should be alone on Valentine's Day, don't you agree? It's positively inhuman."

"I'm not exactly all alone, Marlene," he said. "Eileen Engelhart came out, and now she's trapped here. So—"

"That makes it all the better. I was going to suggest that you put on your boots and mittens and come over here for a hot toddy or a cold quaff, and drink a toast to my favorite saint."

"Over there?" Ralph said, peering at Eileen questioningly. To his surprise, she was nodding affirmatively. "With you and Teddy?" Eileen continued to nod.

Ralph said, "Okay, just for a little while. We'll be there in a few minutes."

When he hung up, he said to Eileen, "What's with you? I thought you wanted to steer clear of Teddy boy."

She smiled a Mona Lisa smile. "I want to see his reaction to your theory of the murder."

"Oh, no!" Ralph cried.

He refused to get into his snow gear until she promised, solemnly, cross her heart, not to say a word about his theory. He didn't know whether to believe her or not. His stomach started to hurt.

17.

"We'll go the back route," Ralph said, leading Eileen to the back porch. The crusted snow on the screening formed a baffle of sorts against the wind. "The plan is to head for the pass through the privet. If we get separated, make your way back to civilization and alert the Saint Bernards. God, listen to that wind whistle."

He pushed the screen door open against an impeding drift. "This is dumb. I'm going back and call the aristocratic Witch of Worcestershire, the baleful Bitch of Buckingham—"

Eileen pushed him from behind. "Keep going."

With head and shoulder braced against the wind, he slogged through the drift to a relatively clear, windswept patch of yard, staggered across it and through the gap in the hedge. Eileen followed in his footsteps. Literally.

He turned to her and said, "Is my nose still on?"

She pinched it with her gloved hand. "Yes."

Before them was the heated pool.

He peered into it. "Instant slush," he said.

She tugged at him. Wisps of steam from the pool enveloped them.

He was still peering at the water. "It does look something like silk, doesn't it?"

"No. Come on. You have ice on your eyebrows."

They stomped onto the Thatchers' back steps. Ralph banged on the door. He had to bang a second time before it was opened by Teddy, dressed in a designer après-ski outfit.

"Mother thought you'd be coming to the front," he said. His tone implied that it wasn't his idea to invite them over.

They were in a long central hall that stretched from the front entrance to the rear. Marlene had transformed it into the gallery of an English manor house. Rich burgundy wall-to-wall carpeting, darkly glistening pieces of furniture, muddy paintings of Thatcher ancestors on the walls, a grandfather's clock.

Marlene came toward them. She was dressed in a dark cocktail gown over which she had pulled on an Irish cable-knit sweater. "Leave your boots there by the door," she said. "How sweet of you to brave the elements to keep a lonely woman company. Teddy, take their jackets. Don't let them drip on the carpet, that's a good boy."

Even with the bulky sweater on she looked elegant to Ralph.

"Which one is Bucky?" he asked.

She looked at him in momentary puzzlement until he gestured at the paintings. "Oh, you can't be interested in those old horse thieves. Come, let us get out of this drafty hall."

She led them into the large living room, filled with stolid furniture. The only thing cheery about it was the fire in the fireplace. He went to it, held his hands out to it, then his butt, as he had seen them do in the movies. "This alone was worth the trip," he said. "Now I'd like to get out of these wet clothes and into a dry martini. I think it was Benchley who said that. Maybe it wasn't. Can anyone tell my why I'm babbling?"

Marlene said, "Whatever the reason, keep it up. I like it."

Eileen said that she too would have a martini. "Stirred, not shaken," she said.

"Atta girl," Ralph said.

At a look from his mother, Teddy went to a sideboard and mixed the drinks. Ralph noticed the stemmed glasses of the mother and son, containing what appeared to be port wine.

Marlene settled more snugly in her chair. "Now let us have a neighborly visit on a wintry evening. Isn't this cozy?"

Ralph didn't think so. The martini was drowned in vermouth and the flavor of olive, and the room was not cozy at all, it was stuffy and vaguely threatening. He made a toast to Saint Valentine, then to Rudolph Valentino, Prince Valiant, and Rudy Vallee. Then he said, "Who's ready for another drink? No, no, let me make it, Teddy."

He made himself a "real" martini, knowing that he was overdoing it, but Lillian wasn't there to say, "You've had enough, Ralph."

He sat back in an overstuffed chair and beamed benignly at the other three. Marlene smiled back. Teddy was sullenly staring into his wineglass. Eileen sat on the edge of her chair, glancing expectantly at Ralph and Marlene as if she were watching a tennis match. She and Teddy carefully ignored each other.

Ralph had one more toast. "To all the people we love."

"Hear, hear!" Marlene touched her glass to her lips.

"There's good news from the hospital," Ralph announced. "Prudence Mannheim's memory seems to be coming back."

"Oh?" Marlene said.

"Yes. Her speech is slurred, but she's a big, healthy woman. She said to me, 'Rudolf and I were going to Germany, isn't that so?' I said yes. She said, 'When I get out, I'd still like to go.' Isn't that great, for a woman who's still halfway between life and death?"

Marlene said, "That *is* wonderful news. Of course, she'll never make it—"

"I wouldn't count on it, Marlene. The doctor says it's an encouraging sign. She might get to Munich, after all."

"She'd be crippled, wouldn't she, poor dear?"

"Probably. But as I said to her, if she didn't make it, Lillian and I'd go in her place. I feel we owe that to her and Rudi."

"Why do you say that, Ralph?" Marlene said. "I can't see any obligation on your part. Oh, his death was certainly tragic, and our hearts go out to Prudence—but *really*."

Ralph blurrily realized he was on dangerous ground.

"You'd have made a good lawyer, Marlene," he said. "When you asked me why, you knew I was talking through my hat. So the answer is, you're right, I *don't* feel an obligation to the Mannheims to go to Germany. And that's the end of that. I think I've had enough to drink, thank you."

Marlene Thatcher looked startled. "I think you just complimented me, but I'm not sure," she said.

Eileen took a sip of her drink and made a face.

Ralph said, "Here, lemme make you a better one. No offense, Teddy, but that wasn't a very good martini."

Eileen let him take her glass. When he returned with her drink, he said, "Who wants to play Twenty Questions?"

Eileen said, "I know a better game."

Ralph saw the look in her eyes and said, "No, sweetie, no."

"It's called, Knock, Knock, Who's the Murderer?"

Ralph said, "It sounds like a totally inappropriate game for Valentine's Day. Wait until Halloween; then we'll play it."

"I never heard of it," Marlene said. "Is this something you made up? It sounds like fun."

"It's lots of fun," Eileen said, rubbing her hands together. "It has ghosts and blood, and we all play detective ... It's only a game, Uncle Ralph. What harm can there be in that?"

Ralph said, "You're playing with fire, kiddo."

"Fire and ice," Eileen said. "Come on, don't be a drag."

Marlene Thatcher leaned forward. "Let's start Eileen's game, and if we don't like it we can stop it. Is that agreeable to everyone?"

Ralph said, "You're not going to like it."

"We'll see," Marlene said. "How does it start, darling?"

"Well," Eileen said. "The first question is for Teddy. Okay, you're a young guy named Raymond, and you've come here from France, and there's an older man here named Kraus who had come from Germany. You've never met him before. One night old Doc Kraus is walking through a snowstorm, and you get in your car and you go after him and you run him over and you kill him. The question is, Why did you do that?"

Teddy looked at his mother then back to Eileen. "This makes no sense. If you're referring to the Mannheims—"

"No, no, it's only a game," Eileen said. "You're Raymond and you killed Doctor Kraus—"

"I have no idea why I killed him. It still doesn't make sense."

"Make up a reason."

"I don't know. Maybe Kraus stole something from me."

"But he has plenty of money. Why would he steal?"

"You know I'm not good at games. Ask somebody else."

"Come on, why would he steal, Teddy?"

Teddy stood up. "Mother, are you willing to play this idiotic game?"

"Sit down, Teddy darling," Marlene said. "I'm interested to find out what Eileen's game is leading up to. As she said, what harm can it do?"

Teddy made a face and sat down.

Ralph said, "I agree with Teddy. Eileen's just making it up as she goes along."

"That's the fascinating part, Ralph," Marlene said. "To see the imagination of a young person at work. Proceed, darling."

Eileen was peering intently at her former boyfriend. "Doc Kraus didn't steal anything from you, did he, Raymond? So there must be another reason why you killed him."

"Maybe I just didn't like his looks, with that stupid beard."

"Come on, Raymond, play the game. That's no reason to kill somebody."

"Maybe he knew a deadly secret about me and was threatening to tell."

"What sort of secret?"

"I came from France? Maybe it was something that happened there."

"But he was from Germany."

"Okay, something that happened in Germany."

"But he came from Germany long before you were born. How could he know something about you?"

Teddy looked at his mother and implored, "*Mother?*"

Marlene said, "Perhaps you should start another line of questioning, Eileen darling. I think Teddy handled himself very well."

"Okay, your ladyship. Do I call you 'your ladyship'?"

"You may call me anything you wish."

"Okay, your ladyship. There's a crazy man named Adelbert who lives on the shore, and Raymond is out on a boat in the middle of the bay. And yet Raymond is able to blow up Adelbert's house and kill him. This question is for Uncle Ralph. How does Raymond do that?"

"Leave me out of this, sweetie," Ralph said. "Why don't you ask Raymond?"

"Because I'm asking you. I bet you can come up with better answers than Teddy did."

"No, no, Teddy's answers were very good. I'd say that Raymond killed Adelbert for the same reason he killed your Doctor Kraus—some dark secret from the past—only I think that Adelbert was a *part* of the secret, a leading part you might say, sort of an actor in it, whereas poor old Kraus didn't know the secret, but Raymond was afraid that he was going to find out and therefore had to be stopped. It's the snows of yesteryear all over again. François Villon asked where the snows were. Well, it seems to me that they're falling on us right now with a vengeance. It's not the wind that's howling out there, it's the vengeance that's been building up inside Raymond howling for satisfaction."

He peered around at the others with the same benign smile on his face. He thought he was being very clever in disarming the vague danger he had felt. "How'm I doing, sweetie? How's that for babbling?"

Before Eileen could answer, Marlene Thatcher said, "Very poetic, Ralph. Snows of yesteryear, howling vengeance. Strong imagery."

"Hoo-hoooo," Ralph howled, sounding more like a train whistle than the keening of the blizzard.

Eileen and Marlene started to speak at the same time. "No, you, your ladyship," Eileen said.

Marlene said, "But what is this deep, dark secret that is raging inside the poor young Frenchman? And how in the world could he kill this Adelhead—"

"Adelbert," Eileen said.

"Thank you, dear. How could he do it from a half mile away? Through mental telepathy?"

"It's interesting that you bring that up, mental telepathy," Ralph said. "One of Eileen's detectives is a mental telepathist. What's her name, Eileen?"

"Er, Phyllis Porterhouse."

"Yes, Phyllis Porterhouse. Oh, I like that name, sweetie. Very good. I'm beginning to like this game. Poor Phyllis gets long-distance messages from the beyond, but sometimes the connection isn't very good, and her predictions turn out wrong. Are they wrong in this case, sweetie?"

"I don't think so," Eileen said.

"For heaven's sake," Marlene said. "Stop beating around the bush. What did this soothsayer say?"

"It's hard to say what a soothsayer says," Ralph said very cleverly. "She sees clouds, rippling silk, things like that. She sees a cloud of evil rising from the past and settling over Savage Point and more specifically over Dover Street. Even as we sit here we're all under a cloud. It has touched us all."

"Yes, and it's dumping two feet of snow on us," Marlene said.

"Hey, that's right. She said it was a white cloud. So her weather forecast was right on the money."

"But what does her weather forecast have to do with how this chap Raymond caused an explosion—"

"It doesn't."

Marlene Thatcher shook her head. "My head is spinning. I think this game is fading away into the white cloud."

"The point is, it wasn't Phyllis Porterhouse who explained how Raymond did it. It was the police."

"Now it's you who's making it up as you go along. Eileen said nothing about the police."

"Stands to reason. Where there's a murder there's the police. Even in a game. The police figure the Adelbert explosion was triggered by remote control."

"From a half mile away?"

"Even so, forsooth."

"You're saying this Raymond fellow had the triggering device on him when he was on the boat. Was he alone on the boat?"

"No, there were eight or nine other people on the boat."

"Preposterous. They would have seen him."

"Not if he had it hidden in the pocket of his jacket."

Marlene Thatcher laughed. "I assume it was your soothsayer, your oracle, who saw this device hidden in the young man's pocket. She has x-ray vision and saw it from— Where was she at the time?"

"I have no idea. And no, Phyllis Porterhouse hasn't claimed she saw the device. But she did touch the fragments of the detonator itself, and she said the triggering thing was buried under water. The police think that means it was chucked into the bay. But Raymond couldn't dump it with all those people around him. Poor Raymond had to hang on to it. What the police didn't know was that Raymond had a swimming pool—"

"Don't tell me. Raymond hid it in the bottom of his pool."

"Yes, in the drain, I'd say."

"Oh, this is delightful," Marlene said. "So the police arrest Raymond on the evidence of a soothsayer. But you haven't said why. What was Raymond's motive? Eileen said this was a crazy man. Was he violently insane? Did he threaten Raymond? Is that why?"

Ralph sighed. His mouth was very dry. "I think I've run out of ideas. I need a splash of something to wet my whistle." He struggled out of his chair, went to the sideboard, and poured some club soda in his glass. "As far as I'm concerned, that's the end of your game, sweetie," he said. "It's time to go."

"O-oh," Marlene said like a disappointed little girl. "You can't stop the game just when it is getting interesting. Perhaps Eileen can tell us why Raymond killed the crazy man. Come on, Eileen, it's your game."

Eileen was peering intently at her. "That's what we came over here to find out, isn't it, Uncle Ralph?"

"Speak for yourself, white girl," Ralph said. "I came over here to give solace to a lovely widow on a wintry night. I trust we have done that—"

"Not enough, dear Ralph," said the elegant widow. "Just one more drink, and then you can go." To Ralph her pleading demeanor was downright flirtatious.

"You twisted my arm, Marlene."

He made himself another martini, poured wine for the two Thatchers. Eileen shook her head.

He held up his glass. "To the gorgeous lady of Dover Street who, like a Rolls-Royce in a used car lot, lends class to the dump!"

Marlene bowed her head, and Ralph thought he had made up a dandy toast, until Eileen finished it off by adding, "Raymond's mother."

The smile faded on the Englishwoman's face.

In the moment of silence that followed, Ralph heard only the baleful howl of the wind in the eaves.

He moved to pull Eileen from her chair. "Come on sweetie, it's time to go."

"No!"

The word from Marlene was a command, and Ralph froze in a bent-over posture.

Then in a mild, motherly voice, she said, "Teddy dear, please bring me the old keepsake from the drawer there. I want to show it to our guests."

Ralph gaped in amazement as the young man retrieved a handgun from a cabinet drawer and brought it to his mother.

"That's a good boy," she said, patting him on the cheek.

18.

She sat erect, composed, holding the gun loosely in her lap.

"It's a Luger, Eileen darling," she said. "The favorite sidearm of the German officer in World War Two. I'm sure Ralph is familiar with it since he fought in that war. It's one of the few keepsakes I have of my father. What sort of keepsakes do you have of the war, Ralph?"

Ralph straightened up. "Is that thing loaded?"

"Of course. What use is a gun if it isn't loaded?"

"It's a nifty-looking gun, Marlene. Now ask Teddy to put it back in the drawer. Guns make me nervous." He glanced at Teddy standing stiffly behind his mother's chair. For the first time there was animation in the face.

Marlene said, "Oh, dear, I don't want to distress you. I simply wish you to continue Eileen's game without the silly names. The two of you have been toying with us as if we were animals in a laboratory. I resent that!"

Ralph made a face. "I see the distress is on the other foot. On behalf of Eileen and myself, I apologize. Now may we go?"

With the gun Marlene waved him to his chair. "First you must finish your story. You've accused my son of killing two people, a crazy man and a bearded psychologist—"

"No," Eileen said. "The beard was put in by Teddy. I didn't say it. He did."

"You're wrong, it was you who said it, sweetie," Ralph said quickly. "I clearly remember—"

"Stop it, Uncle Ralph," Marlene said. "Teddy said it, but it was only part of the game. He was to use his imagination, and he did. Now that Eileen has brought *me* into it as the killer's mother—"

"I did not!" Eileen cried. "All I said was—"

"Darling Eileen, I know what you said, and I know what you meant. It's obvious that the two of you have suspicions about me and my son. Let's get them out in the open. That's all I want. You can understand that."

Ralph and Eileen traded glances; then he laughed. "You've caught us out, Marlene. Eileen and I have been playing a private game. She lost her father and a person who was like a mother to her, and I lost two of my closest friends. It was hard for us to believe that their deaths were just accidents, even though on the face of it that's exactly what they were. Just an awful coincidence—"

"Ralph, you're babbling again," Marlene said. "What was this private game of yours?"

"Well," he said, "we made up stories. Assuming these were murders, we said, who do we know who could have committed them? We listed a few people, and then tried to build a case against them—out of thin air, as they say, because we had no facts. It was a way of getting over our grief. The best case we had was against Todd Gilchrist; he was at the scene, he hated Fred, he set fire to his own house. It's still the strongest case, and I'm convinced that he's the one who killed Fred and Angel. His brain was marinated in alcohol, and there was the time at the club—"

"Your stories are long-winded, Ralph. Get on with it!"

"Well, damn it, you make me feel like Scheherazade. As long as I keep talking, Eileen and I will be safe."

"You forget that Scheherazade's stories had to be interesting. Yours aren't."

Eileen said, "I think we ought to go, Uncle Ralph. We're going to have trouble getting through the snow."

"Not just yet, darling. Your Uncle Ralph is telling a story."

"You have the gist of it, Marlene," Ralph said. "We decided Gilchrist was the one." He smiled weakly.

The sudden rage that took over her body and seemed to explode onto her face was frightening.

Ralph said, "Okay, okay. You want to hear about the others, so okay. The next suspect was Eric Bushman—"

"Let's skip Bushman."

"If you don't want to hear about Bushman, okay. But you have to admit he was a good suspect for Fred's murder. Anyway, we started to build a case against Rudolf Mannheim. And when you look at the early relationship—"

"Mannheim wouldn't kill a fly. He was a weak man."

"He killed your friend Bushman, I'm convinced of that."

Marlene said, "Hah, now we're getting down to cases. Suddenly I have a *friend* named Bushman. Where did I meet this Bushman?"

"It's all just loony speculation," Ralph said in a tired voice. "Wild thought of mine that I never mentioned to Eileen. She doesn't know a thing." He turned to her. "Sweetie, I think you ought to go back to the house now. I'm expecting a call from Lillian. If she rings, tell her I'll call her back."

Marlene was shaking her head. "You really are an amusing person, Ralph, without meaning to. You stay here, Eileen darling."

Ralph said, "Suppose she just gets up and goes."

"I'm sure she wouldn't leave just yet, would you, darling?"

Eileen stared at her without moving.

Ralph said, "Suppose the two of us just get up and go together . . . Let's go, sweetie." He stood up.

"I couldn't let you do that, Ralph."

"Would you shoot us?"

"Would you really go to Europe to check up on us?" Marlene retorted.

"In other words, you would."

"I would get agitated," Marlene said. "And in my agitation the gun might go off accidentally. Just as you might accidentally go to Europe." She waved the gun toward the chair he had been sitting in.

He remained standing. "Do I have your word, the word of a titled English lady, that when I finish telling you the imaginary things I made up about you and Teddy, that you'll let us go on home? And your gun won't accidentally go off?"

"You have my word."

Ralph sat on the edge of his chair.

He said, "What was your maiden name, Marlene?"

She smiled. "What do you think it was?"

"I don't believe I could ever prove it, but I think it was Kohlkopf. If that wasn't your maiden name, my whole story is exploded like Fred's house."

"Wherever did you come up with that name? Was it from your female psychic? Did she find it in the bottom of a teacup?"

"I believe you've heard the name. I got it from the police who got it from the State Department. It was the name of the informant against the Engelhart family back in 1943. The arresting officer was Eric Bushman."

"So that's my connection to Bushman," she said. "This was in Germany, is that correct?"

Ralph nodded. "Munich."

"Und vot makes you tink I vas born in Chermany?" she asked in a comic German accent. She wasn't laughing, however.

"Little things that don't add up to a hill of beans. Just tell us your maiden name wasn't Kohlkopf, and we'll be on our way." He leaned forward as if to stand up.

"What little things?"

"Well, like your name. There aren't too many Marlenes in England, are there? There's Lilli Marlene, Marlene Dietrich, and Marlene Kohlkopf. Do you know what Kohlkopf means in German? I looked it up. It means Cabbage Head. You could have made a fortune

DEATHSTORM 179

selling Cabbage Head dolls if you had thought of it five or six years ago."

She stared at him coldly. "What else?"

"Nothing really. A few expressions that you used, like calling someone, I forget who, a *dumkopf*. But that doesn't mean anything. I've used the word myself. The world is full of *dumkopfs*."

Marlene didn't reply.

He said, "So it doesn't mean anything."

She continued to gaze at him intently.

He said, "You know what really set me off? I remembered how funny Fred acted when he first set eyes on you. Do you remember? He was in our backyard next door, and you were in your yard. And you looked at each other. You stared and stared, both of you. And it seemed that this was not the first time you had gazed at each other that way. Then he disappeared. He didn't want to meet you." He flashed a brief grin. "There you are, an open-and-shut case."

"It's apparent that you have no case at all," she said. "And yet you still believe that I had reason to have my clever son set up explosives and kill the man by remote control."

"Ridiculous, isn't it?" Ralph said.

"Nutty," Eileen said.

He couldn't stop himself from adding, "Of course, Teddy knew the house. He had been there a number of times with Eileen. Probably got the grand tour of the place, right, Teddy?"

Eileen said, "Uncle Ralph, I don't think you should talk anymore. You're making Teddy and his mother feel bad."

"Don't mean to," Ralph said. "Sorry folks. It's the martini that's babbling, not me. It happens every once in a while. Did you know that I was drunk for two years after my first wife died. Margaret her name was. Darn near killed myself. I'm not really an alcoholic, I just sometimes drink too much. Sorry."

Marlene said, "What was Mr. Mannheim going to find out in Munich, Ralph?"

"Nothing, nothing," Ralph said. "Try to find out what happened when Fred threw the grenade at that Gauleiter, what was his name?"

"I'm sure I don't know."

"Giesler! That's the name. I read it in the Shirer book. Tell me, Marlene, what do the White Rose letters mean to you?"

"Nothing special. Should they?"

"If you were Marlene Cabbage Head, they would. I think the little Cabbage Head girl was there."

Eileen said, "*Uncle Ralph!*"

"She was where, Ralph?" Marlene persisted.

"In front of the Fuhrerhaus that day. Fred's grenade missed the Nazi leader and killed some bystanders. At least that's the story I heard."

Marlene shook her head. "I think you heard the story all wrong," she said. "Your dear friend Fred was not aiming at the Nazi leader. He was a Nazi himself, and he deliberately killed some peace-loving people who were there as silent protesters against Hitler's war."

Ralph opened his mouth to speak but was stunned into silence while his brain tried to make sense of what she said. There was no way that Fred intended to kill the bystanders. And yet the facts could fit her interpretation of the incident, just as two eyewitnesses to an altercation frequently came up with conflicting stories.

Before he could stop himself, he said quietly, "You were there, weren't you?"

"You're bloody right I was there!"

Simultaneous to the strangled shout, her whole body clenched, the gun in her lap exploded, glass shattered somewhere. Ralph's senses were assaulted by the roar of the shot and the raw emotion of the voice. He gaped at the other three and saw the shock frozen on their faces.

Marlene looked dumbly at the gun, then slowly followed the direction in which the gun was pointed. Ralph felt the icy air on his face, saw the lacy curtain of the far window billowing inward like a ghostly apparition in the shadows. He pulled his gaze back to Marlene Thatcher.

The hand that held the gun was limp.

A thought formed in Ralph's mind. He lunged toward the gun, reached for it, almost clutched it. Suddenly a strong body was on top of him, and he was pinned, face down on the carpet. Teddy had a knee on his back.

Then Eileen was pushing at Teddy, and he was warding her off. "Stop it, Teddy, I mean it!" she said.

19.

Ralph rolled from under Teddy's knee. The gun was no longer in the mother's lap. It was pointed at him. He lay still. Teddy stood up and forced Eileen back into her chair. Ralph heard the sound of labored breathing, and realized the sound was coming from him.

He looked up into the face above the gun, a face so splotched with red that he scarcely recognized it.

"Mind if I get up?" he asked.

The gun flicked toward his chair. He scrambled off the floor and stumbled to the chair. "Sorry about that," he said.

Marlene appeared to be back in control of herself. She said, "Teddy, love, close the drapes at the window, that's a good boy."

The young man did as he was told, and the sound of the blizzard diminished.

Eileen was glaring at the woman.

Ralph said, "Easy does it, sweetie."

Marlene was shaking her head as if at unruly children. "Now what am I going to do with you two?" she said.

Ralph said, "Why don't you just put that damn gun down and tell us what happened. I'm particularly interested in why you think Fred Engelhart was a Nazi. And then, by God, we're going home."

Marlene Thatcher shook her head sadly. Fatigue was etched on her face. "There seems to be no end to it," she said. "As soon as one duck is knocked down, another pops up in its place. Believe me, Ralph, I did not wish to be in a shooting gallery. I came here simply to exorcise a redheaded devil— Forgive me, Eileen darling, but that's what your father was—"

"You're crazy!" Eileen said.

"Perhaps," the woman said, nodding. "Where were you when you were ten years old?"

Eileen moved a shoulder contemptuously.

"Did you have a horse? Every little girl should have a horse. I didn't have one either. I rode my father's shoulders pretending he was a horse. I had an imaginary whip, and I would wave my arms as if I were whipping him and bounce up and down in my saddle. I was getting too big for that sort of thing, particularly since my father lost his arm in the invasion of Poland.

"My mother thought it was a blessed injury, since after his recovery he returned to his teaching position at university and was saved from being massacred in Russia. He taught English literature. He loved Shakespeare. 'I came to bury Hitler, not to praise him.' He'd recite that at home, not in the classroom. Never in the classroom. Never in the classroom."

She peered at the others and grimaced. "Now it is I who am babbling. It must be catching."

"It's not fatal," Ralph said. "Please babble on."

"What I am doing is thinking out loud," she said. "Trying to clarify my thoughts . . . My father. Yes. He was a very intelligent man. He saw that the German people had invented a monster and deluded themselves that he was leading them to a conquest of the world. Oh, how glorious that dream was! Instead, my father knew at first hand that all Hitler was accomplishing was the destruction of Germany's youth . . . Ach, I sound like a cuckoo in Hyde Park, don't I?"

"Did he get involved in the White Rose thing?" Ralph asked.

"Yes, that. A pitiful affair. Some of the students saw

Hitler in the same light and formed a small resistance group. Needless to say, they were doomed. They tried to distribute leaflets, the poor dears. They were caught, brought before the bloody judge of the People's Court, and executed by hanging.

"No, my father wasn't really involved, but he was a friend of the philosophy professor who was sort of faculty adviser to the foolhardy *kinder*. Kurt Huber was his name. Poor old Huber was strung up along with the students. They missed my father. He bided his time, tried to keep the remnants of the group together. He regarded himself as a conscience, a silent witness to the crimes of the gutter rabble who had become our petty *fuehrers*. The pompous Gauleiter was the most prominent one.

"My father and a few others would go, whenever they were free, and simply stand and stare. They did nothing seditious for which they could be arrested. Rather, they seemed to believe that concentrated thoughts could be transmitted like radio waves; it was all very ridiculous."

She stopped talking, and Ralph saw that for the moment her eyes were unfocused. If he made another grab for the gun, how quickly would she react? Teddy was standing beside him. A glance showed that he was looking at his mother. How quickly would the son react? The gun was still pointing at Eileen and himself. Ralph tensed himself for the leap—

Teddy said, "Mother, you don't have to tell them all this. They were just guessing."

With a slight shudder Marlene Thatcher was back in the present, and Ralph's opportunity was lost.

"That's true, Teddy darling," she said. "But if they go digging in Munich and the Nuremburg records and all the other records—"

"We wouldn't find out a thing," Ralph said. "All this is small potatoes compared to—"

Marlene nodded. Her face was grim. "But can we take that chance? The probability is they could never get enough evidence to convict us. But I couldn't stand going on trial for what they would call murder. The publicity would be intolerable, especially after what happened in England—"

Ralph gave an incredulous laugh. "Don't tell me you killed old Bucky, too!"

"Of course not! But you know the sleazy English newspapers—"

"He died in a fire, didn't he?" Ralph said. "Fires seem to happen around you."

"You sound like the *Evening Standard*," she said coldly. "You see what I mean, Teddy darling. The innuendoes here would be just as bad. The question is, What are we going to do with these two blasted busybodies? We stop one person from going to Europe, and two more pop up like those bloody ducks! Is there no end?"

"Oh, for God's sake," Ralph said. "I've already told you I'm not going to Europe. Mannheim could speak German, I can't. I couldn't get to first base in Munich, believe me! So stop blathering about those damned ducks in a shooting gallery. I have no desire to go to Germany!"

"I've come to know you, Ralph Simmons," she said. "You're a good friend for a person to have. Unfortunately you formed a friendship with the wrong person, and you will avenge his death, no matter what I say."

"That's not true!" Ralph shouted. "All I want right now is to hear the rest of your story about your father's death. I take it that your father was one of those killed by Fred Engelhart's grenade. Tell me about it."

"And you'll still think your dear friend Friedrich was innocent as the driven snow—"

"Try me, for God's sake! I wasn't there, you were. Tell me how Fred was a Nazi killer."

"Did you know that your friend was in the Hitler Youth, and that he—"

"So was Rudi Mannheim and nearly every other teenager in Germany."

"And that he went from there into the Nazi army?"

"Oh, for Christ's sake!"

"He was well indoctrinated, Mr. Ralph Simmons! I'm sure he didn't want you to know that, but he was a fanatical Nazi. That's one of the things you'll find out in Germany if you choose to search far enough. But you won't, will you? You'll only try to find out about the poor Kohlkopfs. You're a fanatic in your own way, admit it."

Ralph peered at her, saw the glint of fanaticism in those eyes, realized their roles had been reversed. Now it was he who had to keep *her* talking—telling stories, so to speak—to ward off the inevitable end.

"So you were on your father's shoulders that day," he said.

"Yes, I was playing horsey," she said. "There were just two other witnesses with us, two of my father's students. We stood to one side of the broad steps in front of the Fuhrerhaus, standing without moving, without expressions on our faces. There was the usual noonday crowd in the Koenigsplatz, but I was the tallest of all. I could look over their heads in all directions. I felt like a queen on my faithful steed, and these were my subjects."

She was obviously reliving the distant moment in her mind, but this time the blond son was watching him.

"Then the Gauleiter was strutting down the steps, putting on his gloves, the walking personification of arrogance. Just to look at him was to want to kill him. Or spit on him, or whatever. We stood there stiffly. I knew he was aware of us, for we had stood witness there before, and once he had asked a flunky to get our names and addresses. Many of those in the crowd were in uniform, so it wasn't unusual that your friend was there in his army uniform. I didn't even notice him until he threw the grenade.

"There was movement in the crowd, of course, people going this way and that. But the motion of the arm in the air was different. I saw it out of the corner of my eye, and I turned. This object was whirling straight toward us, I saw it, and I saw the redheaded soldier stand up from the crowd, staring in our direction. He was looking at me, and I was looking at him.

"I'm sure I must have blinked when the bloody thing exploded. Then my horse was reeling, and a hand came up to try to steady me, my father's hand. All the time I was staring at this redheaded devil until my father collapsed beneath me and my head hit the ground. Even when I was unconscious, I swear to you, that face was in my mind. It has been in my mind ever since. I see it now, Eileen darling, the face of your father."

"But you have to know he wasn't aiming at you, damn it," Eileen shouted. "Why would he want to kill you?"

Ralph said, "You didn't see Bushman knock his arm as he was throwing?"

"Bushman wasn't there," Marlene Thatcher said. "I saw the whole thing, and that bloody killer was aiming at us! He killed my father!"

Ralph sighed. There was no way that he and Eileen could change the woman's haunting memory. But he had to keep her talking.

"Tell us about your mother," he said quietly. "She set out to take revenge, didn't she? Not only on the man who threw the grenade but on his family. Isn't that unusual? They had nothing to do with your father's death."

Marlene sat up straight. "They were ciphers," she pronounced. "They were bystanders without commitment to anything. His father, mother, and sister, nothing, nonentities to everybody except the murderer. When we couldn't catch up to Engelhart, we got back at him through his family. It was my mother's decision. She was not a strong person, but she loved my father very much."

"But how did she know about the family? She knew nothing about the soldier who threw the grenade."

"Ah, that's where my friend Bushman, as you call him, came in," she said. "He was a Nazi. We knew he was a Nazi, but we used him, my mother and I, not the other way around. We didn't know what his motives were, and we didn't care. He was the one who identified Engelhart for us. He showed us a snapshot, and it was true. The face that haunted me was Engelhart's. Then after the war we emigrated to England—"

"Hold it," Ralph said. "Before we get to England, tell us about Engelhart's family. Your mother planted evidence against them, didn't she?"

"Do we have to go into that?" she said in annoyance. "I'm not ashamed of it. This man had taken our family from us. My father was dearer to us than these nothing creatures could have been to him. Their loss would bring him at least a measure of agony. So my mother happily conspired with the Nazi and planted the evidence."

"What evidence could have been so damning as to send them to a concentration camp?"

Marlene Thatcher shrugged wryly. "What else? Some of the White Rose letters my father had hidden away in the eaves. As you can imagine, anything connected to the White Rose affair made the Nazis see red. The trial lasted about forty minutes. I don't know when Engelhart found out about it, but when he did his anguish must have been doubly severe, because if he had any human feelings at all, he must have had great guilt at having been the cause of their deaths. Oh, my heart did bleed for Engelhart." A horrible grin was on her face.

"But that wasn't enough, was it?"

"No, the man still lived. That was intolerable to my mother and me. We formed a pact, my mother and I, that we would track the man down, no matter where or how long, and be his executioner as he was the executioner of my father."

She shook her head sadly. "We didn't foresee that we would have to execute others as well. If it's any consolation, Ralph, I'm sorry about that."

"That makes me feel better," Ralph said. "So you got to England and you married a wealthy Englishman. How'd you arrange that?"

"Oh, come now, you're not interested in that. The little German girl who played horsey on her father's shoulders eventually turned into a good-looking woman who played horsey with an obese middle-aged sybarite. But all that has nothing to do with our present dilemma. I have nothing against you, Ralph, or you, Eileen, but you have deliberately interfered with my life and my son's life. You threaten us, whether you want to or not."

"Did Bucky become a threat?" Ralph asked.

Her eyes opened wider. "That's very perceptive of you, Ralph. When we finally discovered where Engelhart had come to rest—"

"Was it Bushman who told you?"

"Dear me, no. He had no wish to keep up with us, nor we with him. No, there was an article in the *International Herald Tribune*. It seemed that our old grenade thrower had become a famous inventor."

"Was your mother still living?"

"No, poor dear. She never got over the murder of my father. Her mind started to go, and I blame that on your dear friend. In effect, he killed both of my parents."

Eileen said, "You're crazier than I thought." It came out as a sort of growl.

"That's what Bucky said, darling." Marlene turned her eyes to Eileen. "I don't mind what people call me, crazy or whatever, but when they try to interfere with my actions that's when I go positively berserk."

"In a ladylike fashion," Ralph said.

"Of course," she said. "Bucky, the poor old codger, tried to stop Teddy and me from coming to America. He actually claimed I was insane."

"That's when he accidentally incinerated himself?"

"Indeed. He was a very careless man."

Ralph looked at Teddy. "What did you feel about your mother killing your father?"

No emotion showed on the young man's face. "She didn't," he said.

"Don't tell me *you* did it!"

Teddy Thatcher frowned and said nothing.

"Wow!" Ralph said. "You really are a pair of vipers, you two!"

Marlene Thatcher laughed, sending a chill down his spine. "What's the motto of your state of Texas? *Don't tread on me?* It's a cartoon, and there's a snake about to bite a foot. That's us, Ralph, and you're about to get the bite of your life." She laughed again.

Ralph said, "But it seems to be Teddy who does the biting. How did you turn your son into a killer?"

In the instant that followed, the face above the gun became blotched with red, as if the ice in the arteries had broken and blood coursed through. The gun shook, and Ralph thought, Here it comes. It had gotten very cold in the room, and his body shivered.

The trill of the telephone shattered the tension. Mother and son stared at each other.

It trilled again. Marlene Thatcher looked at her wristwatch. "Nobody would believe we were out in this," she muttered. She stood up, handed the gun to her son. "Don't let them make a sound," she said.

She moved across the room to the phone, which was on a mahogany stand near the hall door. "Hello," she sang sweetly.

Eileen said to Teddy, "You *are* a momma's boy. Do you ever wear her dresses?"

Across the room, Marlene was saying, "Why, thank you, Lillian . . . No, they're not here . . . I have no idea—"

Ralph shouted loudly, "Don't shoot, Teddy! The bullet holes would—"

He was aware of Teddy lunging and a guttural sound coming from his throat, then something smashing on his skull, a flash of light, and Ralph Simmons was plunging into icy darkness. Bottomless.

20.

It wasn't that he was comfortable, just that he wasn't uncomfortable. He had no feeling other than that of whirling through darkness, spinning, a lone self in the darkness of space. Curious. He must be moving at high speed, he thought, as he became aware of going through clouds of particles, face first. Very curious. He must take a look at this phenomenon so he could tell Lillian about it. He knew what she would say: "You weren't hitting the particles, Ralph, the particles were hitting you." And he would grouse, "Who's telling this, you or me?"

His eyes opened to slits, and he immediately had to close them. He tried to communicate with the outposts of his body and got no reply. The only thing that seemed to be working was his mind, and after a moment his mind told him he was in deep trouble.

He moved his head to one side and marveled that he could do it. He saw what he had suspected. He was buried in snow, and wind was whipping snow pellets into his face. The funny thing was, he didn't feel cold. Just drowsy, nothing else, just sort of contented.

Then his head started to ache, memory rushed up, and rage broke through the languorous sense of well-being.

He tried to move his arms and legs, and couldn't. He

concentrated on his right arm. "You first, damn it," he said. He imagined that it moved but not much. "Okay, kids," he said to his various parts, "what we're all going to do now is sit up. That oughta be easy. You've done it a thousand times, maybe a million. At the count of three, all together! . . . Three!"

He felt the strain on his stomach muscles. "Good sign," he muttered. Focusing on his arms, he felt his elbows trying to prop up his shoulders. "Atta way to go," he encouraged them.

He was up on his elbows. Sort of. And the small world was spinning. Diagnosis: concussion. Just wait it out.

Then he was sitting up, the wind-whipped snow stinging his face. The spinning slowed, the nausea quieted. All he saw was the whiteness of snow and the blackness beyond. He was in his quilted snow jacket, his knit cap was on his head. He didn't remember putting them on. Someone must have done it for him.

His mind slowly sorted through the circumstances and concluded that he was midway through the process of being murdered. What other explanation was there? He and Eileen were destined to be found after the blizzard abated, perhaps a long time after. It would look as if they had ventured out into the storm and had frozen to death. The only sign of violence would be a bruise on his scalp hidden beneath his hair.

Eileen! Oh, God, was she here too? She had to be. He looked in all directions, saw nothing but snow. His thoughts tumbled in a blizzard of their own—rage at Eileen for playing her games, primitive fear of the unknown, rage at himself for being a smart-aleck, glimpses of his frozen body being discovered (where?), rage shifting to the diabolical lady and her monster of a son, an urge to pray in hopes there really was a personal God (who should have gotten a report from his guardian angel by now), a prayer that it wouldn't be Lillian who found him, a whimpering self-pity—but mostly an all-consuming rage.

Then a sort of mental traffic cop took over, held up

a white-gloved hand, and brought the anarchic thoughts to a halt. Okay, the first priority is to get the hell out of here. But where is "here." Think. Marlene Thatcher's plan, he was sure, was for Eileen and himself to freeze to death. Eileen was known to be visiting Ralph. That being so, it would be a most questionable coincidence if they froze to death at two different sites. Ergo, they should freeze together in the same general area. Conclusion number one: Eileen was close by.

Close by where? Reason it out. He had been rendered unconscious in the Thatcher house, and presumably so had Eileen. Obviously the Thatchers wouldn't deposit them on the Thatcher's own property. Nor would they have lugged the unconscious bodies very far and certainly not out into the street. Ergo (his logical mind liked that word), he and Eileen were in his own backyard! Maybe.

He had to proceed on that assumption.

Though his legs were useless, he was getting increased mobility in his arms, and he could twist and bend his torso. Thrashing about in the snow, using his upper arms and elbows like rudimentary legs, he extricated himself from his snow cocoon. Now taking the full brunt of the wind, his body was being chilled at an accelerated rate.

His forearm hit something solid. Eileen's leg. She was entirely covered with snow. He crawled on top of her body. His hands were as useless as his leg. He frantically swept the snow from her face with his forearms, gouged the snow from her eyes, nose, and mouth with his elbow. He thumped on her head with his dead forearms. She groaned, barely moved her head. "Time to get up, sweetie," he shouted.

He put his tongue to her eyes, warmed her nose with his mouth, brushed her lips roughly with his. He thumped her head again and ordered, "Move it! Now!"

She groaned and said, "No." The voice was faint.

He raised his head and peered around. Nothing but wildly whirling snow. You're in your own damn backyard, he told himself; so which way is the house? He studied each sextant of viewing area. In a slight shift of wind, he thought he saw a pinpoint of light, which was immediately blotted out. The dim forty-watt light on his back porch! Or did he only imagine it?

It didn't matter. He now had a direction.

He started the half-inch-by-half-inch crawl toward where he thought he had seen the light, hooking a forearm under one of Eileen's arms, sliding her with him, sometimes budging her, sometimes not. He grunted with each exertion. His shoulders ached. The grunts turned to sobs. He dug his elbow into the snow one last time, and he didn't move! His cheek was against the screen door—that close to shelter of sorts!—and his fatigued muscles were refusing to work. He had to give them a moment of rest, but if he did that he wasn't sure he could put them back into motion.

His mind was slipping in and out of consciousness. Gotta break through rotten screening, he thought. Just a little push against it with your shoulder. Let go of Eileen for a moment, rise up and fall forward, and the screen will melt away like a cobweb. His body started to rise—

And a boot came down from the sky onto his head, thrusting it deep, deep into the snow, and his exhausted mind gave in to the inevitable. The heavy boot of Fate had stepped in to end his pitiful struggle. His lungs tried to pull in oxygen and got snow.

Then he was plunging through darkness for the second and last time. *Oh, well, who can tell, some'll go to heaven, and some'll go to hell.* Something out of his childhood . . .

21.

This time he was really dead. He was lying on his back with his hands resting on his stomach, the way they lay you out in a casket. This was interesting. *People are awake at their own wake.* He hadn't known that. His eyes were closed, as they should be. He sensed that people were looking at him. Suppose he suddenly popped his eyes open. He probably wouldn't be able to in the order of things, or corpses would be doing it all over the world, causing all sorts of mischief. He popped his eyes open, and he heard Lillian say, "He's coming out of it!"

He went back into it. Not dead. Worse. His brain was damaged. He would sit in a wheelchair, his head rocking from side to side, drool on his chin. Couldn't think. Poor Lillian. Poor Eileen, lying with her hands on her stomach . . .

He found out later that Eileen wasn't dead.

Lillian said, "They thought she was in a coma from exposure or something. Then they found out she was drunk. You were too, Ralph. The doctor said it was the alcohol that saved the two of you."

He thought about it for a long time, finally decided it was funny. He said, "They try to freeze us to death, then they fill us with antifreeze!" He envisioned the scene. Marlene and Teddy pouring warm gin into them straight from the bottle, no vermouth, no lemon twist—barbaric!—to provide a logical explanation for their straying out into the storm: he and Eileen were bombed out of their gourds!

The Burns-and-Allen routine came at a later session. He was George Burns, and Lillian was Gracie Allen. It started out and ended as pure Ralph Simmons, however. Lillian was telling how he and Eileen had been rescued.

Teddy Thatcher had just stepped down on Ralph's head, then for some reason he picked Eileen up in his arms. Lieutenant Joseph Carbine pointed his gun at Teddy, and Teddy dropped her in the snow.

"What did Carbine say?" Ralph wanted to know. "I mean, when he pointed the gun."

"I don't know. I wasn't there."

"I was just wondering if he said, 'Freeze!'"

"I don't know what he said."

"Funny that Carbine would show up at that moment. In our backyard, in a snowstorm, in the middle of the night."

"Not so funny, Ralph. He was right next door asking Marlene Thatcher some questions—"

"Perfectly normal."

"And Eddie Epstein saw some snow by the back door—"

"Eddie was there too? You're kidding!"

"I'm serious, Ralph. Since Teddy wasn't in the house, and his mother didn't know where he was, they thought maybe he'd gone out the back door. So they followed him out, saw footsteps in the snow, and that's how they found you!"

"But why would they do that?"

"Because they were looking for you and Eileen, of course."

"Of course . . . I think I'm missing something. How come they were looking for us?"

"Ralph, please. Why else would they be questioning Marlene Thatcher? To see if you two were okay. Don't you see?"

"I'm a little slow, not very swift, as Eileen says. Tell me again why Eddie and Carbine dropped in on Marlene Thatcher in the middle of a blizzard."

"For crying out loud, Ralph! When I called Eddie and told him what I'd heard on the phone—"

His attempt to laugh turned into a coughing fit.

"Don't do that, Ralph. You have pneumonia."

"Great. What else have I got?"

"Just the concussion, that's all."

Eileen was able to visit him when she was released from the hospital. "You bit my nose," she said. He told her it was a tribal custom.

He said, "You know what I can't get straight in my mind? What came over your father to toss the grenade."

"He always acted on impulse, you know that."

"And he just happened to have a grenade in his pocket? No, he took that grenade with him. He must have planned it at least a day ahead. Here was a typical German kid of his time. Hitler Youth. Army. And without telling anybody, he goes and does that. How do you explain it?"

Eileen said, "I understand it, but I can't explain it. He just did."

Lieutenant Joseph Carbine came with a video cameraman to get Ralph's statement.

Ralph said, "You know, I kinda liked that crazy lady."

"I know what you mean, Simmons," Carbine said. "She graciously offered me tea."

"You should have held out for Scotch."

"This was in the interrogation room at the station. There was no tea there."

"Over the edge?"

"She kept insisting someone named Bucky set fire to himself. Never heard of anyone named Engelhart."

Carbine said they were charging the mother and son with mass murder. "'Thanks to you, we found the remote control in the pool."

"Thanks to me?"

"You were a babbler, Simmons. A mumbler. Mumbling about a silk pool. It was in the drain wrapped in plastic."

"How about the explosives?"

"One of his friends at engineering school was an Iranian. We're trying to track that feller down."

"You think you'll have enough evidence?"

"Damn right." Carbine had a grim look on his face. "He's a very pretty boy. He's not going to enjoy himself at Attica."

"Jesus," Ralph said.

Penelope Potter summoned Eileen Engelhart to her house.

"You must decide what you wish to do with your father's land. I can get you half a million dollars for it. That's a lot of money, young lady. I had a vision of the new house, one not so outrageous as—"

"No, no house," Eileen said. "Uncle Ralph and I talked about it. I wanted to design a monument to my father, and Uncle Ralph said the best monument would be a garden. So that's what we're going to do. Cover it over with topsoil, form terraces down to the water, and plant the whole thing with roses. The best breed of white roses. You'll be able to see it from as far away as Co-op City. The Garden of the Good German. How does that sound?"

Penelope Potter shook her head. "What a waste," she said. "What a terrible waste." She had seen the new house so clearly—